Through It All

Shelly Kew

Cicely, my friend,
Thank you for your
continued support!
Shelly Kew

This book is a work of fiction. Names, characters, places and events other than those clearly in the public domain are a product of the author's imagination. Any depictions or resemblance similar to anyone alive or deceased are purely coincidental and not intended by the author.

Edited by Guernica D. Williams
Cover art by Germancreative

Published and printed in the United States of America

ISBN 9781095679494
First print, May 9, 2019

This one is dedicated to the Fab 5... Ashley, Devon, Lamaria, Cierra, and Courtney.

I hope I have shown you that no matter what you go through or how it bleak it may look, anything is possible.

"In every crisis there is a message. Crises are nature's way of forcing change — breaking down old structures, shaking loose negative habits so that something new and better can take their place."

Susan L. Taylor

Sunshyne

Jeanette Morris, also known as Sunshyne, has been working to get her life back in order. After the devastations and tragic events that came crashing down on her less than a year ago, she could now see light at the end of the tunnel. Sunshyne had started seeing her life from a different perspective after discussing her issues with Pastor Collins and attending Bible study regularly. Instead of a *woe is me* attitude and wallowing in her misfortunes, she'd begun to look to God even more for her strength. She started living with purpose and not for everyone else around her.

Far too long she depended on Jeanette Morris to work things out in her life and had stopped trusting Him. When things became too overwhelming and she couldn't handle what was coming at her, it was *Dear Lord, please help me*. She did not want to miss Bible study and was trying to get out of the shop in order to make it but her last customer wanted to talk about the trip she had just returned from. Instead of rushing her, Sunshyne went ahead and cleaned up while Rhonda told her all about it.

"Girl, Paris is such a beautiful city. You have to go there one of these days," she said talking with pure excitement in her voice.

"I just might make it there one day," Sunshyne half promised herself. She would love to visit the City of Love, as it is commonly referred to, but she hates being in the sky for a long time and is nervous about places overseas.

"When you go, don't worry about riding up the Eiffel Tower. Most people usually make sure they put that on the top of the list. The view is great, but you can see the same view from other places with less hassle."

That really didn't matter to Sunshyne, she was terrified of heights anyway.

"I recommend you take a river boat cruise at night. The Eiffel Tower is absolutely beautiful when it's lit up." You could see Rhonda's mind go back to her boat ride. "Let me show you the suite he had us staying in." She pulled her cell phone out of her Louis Vuitton tote hobo bag.

Rhonda opened her photo app to show Sunshyne her luxurious room. The room was decorated with 18th-century inspired furniture. As they were looking at the marbled bathroom, they noticed a moving truck pulling up to the building across the street. It had been vacant for over a year since the previous owners retired to the south and took their mom and pop shop with them. There had been a crew working for the past few weeks, and since they had paper up to the windows you couldn't tell what was going on inside. No sooner than the moving truck parked, a black Cadillac XT5 pulled alongside two more cars. The ladies stood in the window to watch what was happening. Maybe now they would get the chance to see. The guy driving the moving truck got out and used a key to open the door.

Rhonda turned to Sunshyne, "What do you think they are doing over there?"

"I am not sure, but it looks like we are about to find out soon enough," Sunshyne replied.

"I guess Pastor Collins won't see you tonight."

"Nope. I need to see what's going down around here. See who my neighbors are gonna be." They both laughed but turned their attention back to the activities going on across the street.

The men who got out of the cars helped to carry items from the moving truck into the building. It was mostly furniture, couches, chairs, and tables, but the ladies couldn't figure out what the place was going to become.

"I say it's gonna be a hookah lounge or maybe just a lounge." Rhonda was the first to give her opinion.

"I think a hookah lounge is a good idea. It seems like those are popping up more these days, and we don't have one close. I can't tell what it will be by the furn..." Then she saw what she knew could only be a stylist or barber's chair. She couldn't believe they were moving in to open another salon right across the street. Who the hell did they think they were coming into their territory? As soon as her thoughts entered her mind, the guy in the passenger seat of the Cadillac truck pointed to her shop. Then he and another guy started walking towards them. Sunshyne and Rhonda jumped from standing in front of the window like they had been busted doing something wrong. Sunshyne got it together real quick. She opened the door, and they stepped out to greet them.

Sunshyne had not been able to get a full view of him from across the street but she saw how stunning he was as soon as she opened the door.

"Hi. My name is Kody, and this is my little brother, Niko."

Kody was short. She was sure he couldn't be more than 5'7" with wide shoulders. His light brown complexion was as smooth as caramel syrup being poured on a sundae. His eyes were the color of a deep, rich, brown coffee bean with reddish flecks, and his black curly afro was very short and neat.

Niko cleared his throat and clarified things. “Younger brother.” The ladies understood there was nothing little about Niko. He was much taller than Kody and looked like he weighed well over 300 pounds.

Sunshyne had a hard time getting her thoughts together. “Hi. My name is Sunshyne Jeanette.”

“Nice to meet you, Sunshyne Jeanette.”

Rhonda stepped in. “Actually, her name is Jeanette, and my name is Rhonda.”

Kody extended his hand to Sunshyne, and she politely shook it never taking her eyes off of him—not even to acknowledge his brother. Rhonda shook Niko’s hand.

Sunshyne finally came out of her trance. “I am part-owner of *Kuts and Kurls*. I’ve been watching to see what’s been going on over there. I was wondering when someone was going to finally move in. I haven’t seen you around here at all. What is it that’s opening? Where are you all from? Are you the owner?”

Niko turned to Kody like the ladies weren’t standing there. “Man, I don’t know if she is the owner of this shop, or if she’s working undercover.” Both men laughed out loud.

“We lived in Rufus King, a quaint little neighborhood of Milwaukee. Our shop recently burned down, and it started becoming just a little to hood for us. We wanted to relocate, and a partna’ of ours told us about an opportunity in the beautiful City of Glenmont. He said the area was a great place for small businesses. He also said the sun always shines on Glenmont, and I have been pleasantly surprised by the beautiful weather we’ve had since I’ve been down here.”

Even though the calendar said it would be winter for a few more weeks, the weather had been refreshingly warm. Normally spring didn't come to this area until the end of March or April, but for the past couple weeks the sun blanketed Glenmont causing the trees and flowers to bud earlier than expected.

Now it was the ladies turn to laugh.

"What's so funny?" the brothers spoke in unison.

"Well, my nickname is Sunshyne with a *y* instead an *i*. I guess as long as I'm around there will always be sunshine."

"Maybe my guy was on to something. In that case, I hope you will be around for a while. I love the sunshine." He gave her a teasing wink.

"Hopefully you will too. I mean, hopefully your shop does well for you."

"Well, we better get back and make sure they ain't broke nothin'. It was nice meeting you ladies, and I'm sure we will speak again. Before I forget, do you mind if I give you some flyers for our grand opening?"

"No. Not at all," Sunshyne said.

Kody ran across the street to grab the flyers while Niko stayed to get more acquainted. Kody came back with the flyers and handed Rhonda one, and gave the rest of the stack to Sunshyne.

"Thanks. Make sure you give one to your man." He noticed she wasn't wearing a ring and figured there was no husband.

"I don't have one of those right now, but I will definitely make sure to tell my brothers." Sunshyne made sure it was clear. She noticed a small glint of delight in his eyes or at least she hoped she did after she told him.

"Alright. You ladies have a good night and be safe out here."

"You too." With that, Kody and Niko were headed back to the shop. Halfway across the street Niko turned to his brother, "My bro is smitten. I seent it all over your face." Kody gave him a playful nudge with no real effect and went back to supervisor mode.

Sunshyne and Rhonda waited until they had gone back across the street. Rhonda turned to her, "Somebody is sweet on Kody. I could hear it all in your voice."

"Well, let's hope he could too."

Rhonda gave her a high five, "I know that's right."

"Let me get back in here and finish cleaning so I can pick up my children." The ladies went back in and Sunshyne swept the pile of hair that she left. She locked up, and the ladies went to their cars.

Kody stood in the doorway watching her leave. He couldn't wait to make love to *the beautiful Sunshyne Jeanette* or whatever else she would let him call her.

***

Sunshyne stopped at 7-11 to grab a couple of Arizona green teas, and then called her mom to see if the kids were ready or if anybody wanted something from the store. Her mom answered almost immediately, "Hello."

"Hey, Ma Dear."

"Hey, Baby. Is Bible study done already?"

"I didn't get to make it. You remember the shop Mr. and Mrs. Berry used to own?—Some guys remodeled it and turned it into a barbershop, and my last customer and I welcomed them to the neighborhood. I realized Bible study was half way through by the time I got ready to head out and figured I'd would just go home. What are the kids doing? Y'all done baking cookies?"

"Child. These kids know they get me every time. We were *only* supposed to make chocolate chip cookies, but then MJ and Mariah wanted peanut butter. I'm all baked out for another month at least. Hopefully they are too. Maia and Mariah bathed and are getting ready for bed. MJ just got in the shower. They asked if they could stay the night, and of course Daddy and I agreed. You don't have to come get them tonight. Daddy or I will take them to school in the morning."

"Are you sure, Mama?" Sunshyne asked.

"Yea, baby. There is no need to get the girls out of bed. They will be fine." Her mama enjoyed whatever time she got to spend with her grandkids, even if it was breakfast at the table in the morning.

Sunshyne thanked her mom and drove home thinking about Kody and where things might lead.

Renae

Renae woke to her cell phone ringing. She thought she was dreaming at first so she didn't move right away. She realized it was the playtime ringtone she set on her cell phone. She rolled over and saw that it was only three in the morning. She had to be up in a few hours and could not understand who would be calling her at this time of morning. She immediately became worried. She prayed it wasn't about her daddy. She jumped up and grabbed her phone and saw it was Paul's baby sister, Tanya. It had been several months since she had spoken to her. They remained tight after Paul died but she hadn't spoken with her in a while. It was weird for her to be calling her let alone at this time of morning. Ruben went to the washroom when she reached to grab her phone.

She answered the phone sounding half sleep and a little puzzled, "Hello?"

"Nae. What are you doing?" Tanya yelled and slurred into the phone. This is why she was calling at three in the morning. She was drunk.

"Do you know what time it is? I am doing what most people do who have to go to work in the morning. What do you want? Is everything okay?"

"Girl. I just had to call you. Mama and Kenyata told me not to. They said you never really loved Paul and that you are glad he is dead. I know that is a lie. I know you loved him with all you had in spite of everything he did. I just wish you and him could...." Renae knew she didn't want to hear anything she was about to say after that. Plus, it was enough trying to understand her.

"Tanya, it's three a.m. What do you want? I have to be up for work in a few hours." Renae was beginning to get irritated.

"The police called Mama last night to inform her they had gotten a break in the investigation. Somebody had finally come forward with some information. There's a lady who says she saw some people driving away from the Forest Preserves around the time Paul's car was burning." Her voice shook like she was about to cry.

A nervous pain filled Renae's stomach and rose to her chest. She tried to hide the disappointment when she spoke. "That's good. Did they say what kind of car it was?" She tried to remember what kind of car Rufus drove that day. Ruben walked out of the bathroom. Renae put her finger up to signal for him to give her a minute. She continued the conversation with Tanya.

"No. They didn't give her much information but said they would come by the house tomorrow to speak with her some more. Well, I guess later today. Nae, I hope this will lead them closer to my brother's killer. Whoever the coward or cowards were that shot him in cold blood, need to die too." She was crying. Renae felt bad for her. She never wished the pain of losing a loved one on anybody, but she really didn't miss Paul at all. Was she glad he was dead? No. Had she been losing any sleep over it? That was a negative as well.

"Tanya, you need to get home. You shouldn't be out by yourself in this type of condition. Text me when you make it home and I'll give you a call later to see how you are. Maybe we can get together and figure out who the driver was after you get more information."

"Okay. I will. Stay strong, Nae. Hopefully all this will be done soon. Love you, girl."

"I will. Get home safe." She ended the call.

Renae turned to face Ruben.

"What was that all about?" he asked.

"That was Paul's baby sister. She said someone came forward and identified a car leaving the Forest Preserves where they found Paul's body and car. She didn't have much information, but I told her I would call her back. Baby, I am getting nervous all over again. I hope everything will be alright."

"Don't worry about a thing. Everything is going to be just fine. *We* are going to be just fine." He turned off the light and moved in closer to hold her to make her feel more at ease. “Since you gotta be up in a little while anyway, how about I help ease your tension. I got something to help take your mind off all of this." He slid down under the covers and raised her nightgown. She had a million thoughts racing in her head. They started dwindling fast as his firm but gently tongue flicked her pearl.

Sunshyne

They had been working very hard at *Close Cuts*, the new barbershop opening across the street. Sunshyne and Kody had a few conversations in passing but she welcomed his refreshing conversation. It was good to be able to have adult conversation without expecting anything—at least for now. She wanted more from him but didn't want to rush anything. She had learned that if it was meant to be it would come, and she shouldn't do anything to mess with it. *Close Cuts'* grand opening was tomorrow. They were offering free cuts for any young man accompanied by a male adult. Kody told Sunshyne it was a way to get the men to bring a younger brotha with them, but they were not going to turn any kid away. He and his brother made it a point to stop in the salon regularly and other small businesses on the block to simply say good morning. During one of their conversations Kody told Sunshyne, "I look to plant roots in a community if I am doing business. I want everyone to know that we didn't open our shop simply to make money. Of course, we want to be successful, but we also want to give back when we can. The grand opening will be the beginning of many ways we plan to invest. I feel that is important." This morning was no different. Sunshyne was working on her second customer when he stopped by.

He came into the shop looking like he just came off tour with Run-DMC. He had on a black and white Adidas track suit, white and black shell toes and a Milwaukee Bucks baseball cap. The only thing he was missing was a *dookie* chain.

"Good morning, ladies."

Almost in unison, the entire shop gave a cheerful, *Good morning*.

"How are you ladies doing today? I hope you've told all the men you know about our grand opening tomorrow. If you have sons, nephews, or little brothers, make sure they get over there as well." The entire time Kody did not take his eyes off Sunshyne.

A couple of the women attempted to get his attention with questions, but his focus was locked in on Sunshyne. Lollie and Meechie both noticed how mesmerized he was with the other owner of the shop. They would definitely give her some grief about it later. Finally, he walked over to Sunshyne's chair, "I was wondering if you would have time for lunch later."

She was a bit taken back by his assertiveness but welcomed it at the same time. "Sh... sh... sure. I will have a break around one-thirty if that works for you."

"That is perfect. I'll be back over to get you. Ladies, enjoy the rest of the day and I hope to see some of you tomorrow." He stopped to answer the questions the ladies had for him earlier. He left the shop with a smile plastered across his face, feeling a small sense of victory.

Lollie couldn't wait for him to make it across the street before she started, "Uh oh. Looks like Jeanette has an admirer. He ain't wastin' no time with you girl. He's only been on the block a few days and already needs a little *sunshine* in his life." Meechie walked past the front desk to go the shampoo area and high-fived Lollie. Throughout the shop you could hear, *Yes, girl*, or *You go, girl. He's a fine brotha right there, you better go, girl."*

Sunshyne continued curling her client's hair and smiled. "Don't you ladies worry, I got this."

***

Before Sunshyne could finish her last client for the morning, Kody was sitting patiently waiting for her. When she finally turned to notice him, she held up her hand to suggest that she needed five minutes. He gave her an obliging nod and went back to taking care of whatever it was in his phone. About ten minutes later Sunshyne was ready to go. She told Lollie that Ms. Washington would be in around three o'clock, to shampoo her and put her under the dryer if she arrived before she got back. They couldn't go too far because she didn't like not being there for her clients when they arrived. She suggested Noodle & Company in Old Orchard Mall. She figured it was a short ride and it wouldn't take long to eat. When they walked out of the shop, he walked over to a silver Nissan Maxima, and opened the passenger door for her. She wondered how many cars he owned.

He must have read her mind because before they could pull off the block good enough, he said, "This is my car. The truck belongs to Niko."

"What made you come out and say that? Feeling a bit of guilt?"

"Naw, I saw a hint of perplexity on your face and wanted to clear it up for you. I don't want to start out this relationship with you thinking I'm one of those brothas with extra cash flow, if you know what I mean."

"Relationship, huh? Don't you think you're being a little presumptuous? We haven't even had a first date and already you talking about a relationship. Do I need to be worried? I don't want to become the topic of a Lifetime movie."

He let out a little chuckle, "No, sweetheart. You don't have to worry about that but you are a very attractive woman and I would like to get to know you better. Maybe *relationship* was a bit much. Still, I don't want you thinking I'm more than just a barbershop owner and that I might make an appearance on any episodes of *Cops* since we're talking about upcoming roles," he said with a sly smile.

"That's good to hear. You have everything in place and ready to go for the grand opening tomorrow? I managed to talk my brothers into trying you out. You know how you men are about your barbers."

"Yep, the same way you ladies are about your hairdressers. I believe we have everything in order for the most part. Niko is taking care of last-minute stuff. We were having some electrical issues, and he is there with the electrician now. Hopefully, by the time I get back it will be taken care of. If not, we will work around it. That's enough about me and the shop. Let's talk about Ms. Sunshyne."

"There isn't really much to talk about."

"So you're a modest one, huh? I can't believe that. There has to be something worth sharing."

"You already know I'm part owner of the shop. I'm born and raised here. I have three children. Never married. Didn't go to college. Graduated cosmetology school and worked at a few shops before meeting Meechie. We worked together at a shop for a while where we brought in about seventy-five percent of the clientele, so we decided we would try opening our own, and here we are. I love house mus..."

"What you know about house music?"

"Man, don't play with me. What don't I know about house music? What do you know about it?"

"I know about Club LaRays, Medusas, AKA, The Warehouse. I know I'm at the Chosen Few picnic they have in the city every year. What else do you need for me to prove I know my ish."

"Ok. I guess you know a little somethin, but I can't believe you come to the picnic every year and I haven't had the pleasure of running into you. I am there every year myself."

"Well we're here now so let's make the most of it."

They pulled directly in front of the restaurant into the mall's parking space. As Kody opened the door for her and as Sunshyne entered the building, she thought that even though they'd had brief conversations he was easy to talk to and wouldn't mind having plenty more conversations with him.

Renae

Renae had tried reaching out to Tanya a few times over the last couple days. She thought she would have called by now to tell her what the police said. She wondered if Tanya thought she too had something to do with Paul's murder after the police gave them the information they had. Ruben kept trying to tell her not to worry about anything. He said he had it all under control, but she couldn't help herself. After Paul went missing and after his body was found, the police questioned her and Ruben a few times but determined there wasn't any evidence connecting either of them. Even still she didn't know what exactly happened, but she knew for sure something happened that day Ruben said everything was going to be alright. There was always a chance they would find something to connect Ruben and Rufus.

Her phone rang as she left work and walked to the parking garage. "Hello."

"Hey Nae. Girl, I know I was supposed to have been called you but I ain't had my phone since the day I talked to you. Mama and I just left the Sprint store. She did not want me without a phone any longer." Tanya was a sweet girl, but she was also very reckless. She was the baby of the family and gave their mother the most problems. Renae understood why her mother would get her a phone. She had two children, and she regularly disappeared for days at a time.

Renae didn't feel like getting into what happened to her phone. All she wanted to know was what happened when the police came. "Yea, girl. I thought you had forgotten about me or your mama, and Kenyata had convinced you that I was involved."

"Girl, bye. I told you before I know you loved Paul and I don't ever think you would have done no shit like that."

"So, did they come to the house? What did they have to say? I hope it was good news because no matter what I want whoever did this to get what they have coming to them. Nobody deserves what happened to your brother."

"No they don't. The police told her they were looking for an older black Nissan or Toyota with tinted windows and had a partial license plate number. The lady *thought* there were two people in the car but wasn't sure if they were men or women because the windows were too dark. The police also saw he had called Boney. They referred to her by her government name, but I knew who they were talking about. They also said he had been texting the chick Monica. They spoke to Monica and were convinced she had nothing to do with his murder." This wasn't a shock to Renae because Sunshyne had already shared the information Richard had told her. This was Glenmont, news didn't take long to travel. A few people screenshot Monica and Paul's baby and sent it to her. Even though she didn't know he had been sleeping with Boney too, nothing about who his partners were came as a shock to her anymore.

Tanya's voice started to crack, and she could barely get the rest of her words out. "They told Mama that they had questioned Boney a few times and were still looking into her but didn't have enough to charge her on anything. I'm just glad it's the Elgin Police looking into it and not Glenmont. If it was Glenmont's finest they would have given up a long time ago like they do so many other murders that take effort in solving. Mama is starting to feel like they will never find out who did it. Things seemed promising but she felt the evidence they had was flimsy now."

Renae knew it wasn't going to be easy-and she knew Tanya knew that as well. There had been plenty of other deaths that had gone unsolved. She still tried to comfort Tanya. "Girl, they will find out who did. At least they haven't stopped questioning people and investigating. Like you said, it's a different jurisdiction working his case. I'm sure they will get to the bottom of this." All this time Renae prayed that they didn't even come close. She knew what happened was wrong and they should go to jail but she could not see Ruben going to jail even if it was for her own selfish reasons.

"Alright, Nae. I gotta call you back. Maybe we can get together one day and catch up. I know the owner at Buster's over on Sheridan. We can hang out and have a few drinks on him."

"That sounds cool. Let me know when you will be around and we can work something out," Renae replied knowing full well she wasn't gonna ever see Tanya unless she bumped into her somewhere.

They hung up, and Renae texted Ruben, *Hey Mr. B. What you doin*? She sat in her car wondering how soon it would be before the Elgin police figured out who Paul's killer was or if the secret she held would never see the light of day. Ruben hadn't texted her back, and she was close to her daddy's, so she decided to go visit him.

Sunshyne

The weekend was almost over and Sunshyne was exhausted. She had a full book on Saturday. When she left the shop, she and Michelle had taken the kids to Jump Zone. Since the weather was surprisingly warm for March, Carlton had hamburgers and hot dogs on the grill for them. They hung out at their house until one in the morning so the kids spent the night and Sunshyne went home. Michelle texted her this morning to tell her she would let the kids sleep in and that she could pick them up after church. Sunshyne was dragging but knew she wouldn't miss church. After the scare with Maia and everything else she went through last summer she promised herself and God that she would never miss a Sunday at New Light unless it was absolutely necessary. Sunshyne got herself in gear by getting ready for the eleven o'clock service. The Light had been off the chain for the past few weeks and she knew today would be another awesome Sunday.

She pulled into her trusty parking spot down the block and walked to the church with Ms. Edgars and her grandson. "Good morning, beautiful. How are you this morning?" Ms. Edgars was one of her favorite elders at the church. She was always pleasant and never seemed to have a scowl or a frown on her face.

"I am wonderful. How are you? Hey Micah. How you doing today? Are you going to play baseball again this year?" Micah let out a soft *Hi* and nodded his head. Sister Edgars got on him but Sunshyne told her it was alright.

"Eight o'clock service was good today. I can't wait for the next one. How is your baby girl doing? She looks to be doing a lot better these days."

"Yea. It was pretty scary at first, but she is doing great now." They walked into church greeted by one of New Light's smiling ushers.

"Good morning, ladies. Praise the Lord and happy Sunday to you," she said with much excitement in her voice. Sunshyne spoke and hugged a few people before finding her way to her seat. Michelle and Carlton had already made it, and her parents were there as well. She walked over, greeted them, and gave them a hug, "Good morning Mommy, Daddy."

They both replied, "Hey sweetheart." It almost sounded like they were in stereo. Her parents visited a few times but still hadn't joined. They decided to visit between New Light and First Baptist, the church Desiree attends with Jerome. After the morning ritual for New Light—the choir marching in, devotion, and the ministry of song, Pastor Collins went to the podium. "Good morning, Saints. Thank you to the ministers, officers. This morning I am going to take a break, and we will have the privilege of hearing from one of the other ministers on the pulpit."

He introduced Minister Harrison and she took her place at the podium. "Praise the Lord, Saints. Praise the Lord. Go with me to II Corinthians 5:17. It is a familiar passage—at least familiar to those who read God's word, but that's not what we're here to talk about. Today I want to discuss surviving, being a survivor of your circumstances and the situations life has dealt you. In II Corinthians Paul writes, and I'm reading from the New Century Version, '*If anyone belongs to Christ, there is a new creation. The old things have gone; everything is made new!*'"

Sunshyne knew church was gonna be short today. None of the assistant pastors ever took as long as Pastor Collins. They gave their message and kept it moving. Minister Harrison instructed the congregation to turn to their neighbor and tell them, *I've got a story to tell. I've got a testimony.* "All of us have gone through something and come out of it. We are survivors of illnesses, physical abuse, or emotional abuse, to name a few. You have been through it and now you are on the other side. When you come out on the other side you shed some, if not all, of what kept you in bondage. You got rid of depression, heartache, and unhealthy thoughts. You overcame what you endured and became a new person. You have a new walk, a new talk, and a new attitude. You are no longer that same person."

Members of the church stood up on their feet and to give her a few *amens*. She continued her sermon, "Survivors condition their spirit to be able to sustain them to the end of the journey. We must be conscious of the spirit of God. Surviving brings you to a different place, and it is God's spirit along with the sensitivity of our heart that continues to heal us once we have overcome and in a new place. There are times when we wonder why we've had to undergo some of the stuff we've faced. Well church, if you don't go through how will you ever learn to lean on the Lord? You go through so you can learn to lean on Him. I don't know about you, but I've been through more than one situation or another where I know for sure it had to be the Lord. I can hear Mahalia Jackson singing, '*Lord, Don't Move the Mountain*'. You're gonna have to learn how to tunnel your way through. You have prayed for Him to move them out of the way but He is telling you that you need to rely on His word and learn about the power He holds."

Minister Harrison finished her sermon by assuring them that in order to get their victory they will have to let go of some of the people in their lives.

"There are some people you are connected to who are interfering with your testimony. Proverbs 13:20 tells us, '*Whoever walks with the wise becomes wise, but the companion of fools will suffer harm*.' You can't expect everyone to go where you're going. You have to learn that you cannot shout in victory if you are connected to defeated people. Survivors know when to move on and go where God has directed you. Remember that wherever He directs you, He will protect you. If you pay close attention, He will show you who to get rid of and when to get rid of them. Praise Him in anticipation of your victory. Shout and let others know that with God you are a survivor."

Minister Harrison finished up her sermon and opened the church for anyone who wanted to join. No one came forward so she gave the benediction and dismissed service.

***

As Sunshyne was on her way to her car, Richard pulled up beside her.

"Hey Ms. Lady. How have you been?"

Sunshyne was a little shocked to see him. He didn't really have a reason to be on this side of town, at least not that she knew. She had not spoken to him in quite a while and didn't know what he was doing. She still found it odd and was a little apprehensive, and he could hear it in her voice. "I'm good. What you doing over this way?"

"Well damn. No, how are you, or it's nice to see you? That's not the response I was looking for but my daughter is in the play over at Morton Center. She has a couple solos," Richard was beaming from ear to ear.

"I guess all those lessons are paying off. I hate to be so short, but I have to get to Michelle's to pick up my children. Enjoy yourself!"

Sunshyne turned to walk to her car, “What did you do last night? Why are the kids at Michelle’s?” Richard was asking one too many questions for her.

She looked at him, eyebrows wrinkled. “Have fun at your daughter’s play.” This time she didn’t wait for him to say a word and walked to her car. He no longer had any rights to question her about anything.

***

Sunshyne picked up the kids and went home so they could get cleaned and dressed. Sunshyne laid across her bed reading a weight loss transformation book, *Balancing the Scale: What I Gained by Losing* written by Tiffini Holmes. Even though her journey was different from the author’s, Desiree felt her sister would benefit from the experiences she shared. While she was reading she received a text from Kody.

Hey beautiful. How are you today? Been thinking about you and thought I’d see what you were getting into today.
Hey sir. I’m doing pretty good. I’m spending the day with my children. Promised them I would take them to see Paul Blart Mall Cop. Then we’ll probably grab something to eat. How are you today?
I’m good. Have fun with the kiddies. Maybe if ur up to it we can link up later.
That sounds good. I’ll let you know when we’re done.

Maia busted in her room, “Mommy, we’re ready and I’m starting to get hot. So please let’s go.” Maia was standing there in her baby blue North Face fleece jacket.

“How long have you had your coat on? Never mind. Let’s go.” The other two were sitting on the couch on their phones playing games or on social media as usual. Sunshyne grabbed her keys and off to the movies they went.

On their way Michelle sent her a video of her trying to skate. She said the Morton Center offered skating today and Carlton thought it would be a good idea to take the kids. Plus, Michelle loved to roller skate back in the day. There was not a Friday night when Michelle wouldn't drag her to The Rainbo. She didn't skate but you really didn't have to skate to enjoy yourself. It was a party no matter what. Sunshyne told Michelle not to try too many of the old tricks because she ain't that young anymore and she'd hate for her to be laid up somewhere. After she finished texting Michelle, she remembered Richard told her he was going there to see a play. Why did he feel the need to lie to her? She knew for sure they weren't doing both but she let it go and went into the movies.

Renae

Renae had not spoken to Ruben since Saturday afternoon. They had gone to Dengeos for lunch and then he had errands to run. It was odd that she had not heard from him because if they did not talk, they texted regularly. The only other person she knew to contact was Rufus, and he wasn't answering either. She hadn't called his mom or sister before she went to church; she didn't want to worry them yet for no reason. She knew they had wild parties at the club that didn't end until after sunrise sometimes, so she figured she'd wait until she got out of church to start calling. She had barely got settled into her dad's, and waiting for Ms. Loretta to finish Sunday dinner when Ruben finally called her.

She didn't even say hello when she answered the phone. As soon as she slid the button on her Galaxy S6, she went in on him. "Where have you been? Why haven't you been answering my calls? I know you saw me calling AND texting you yesterday, and this morning!" Her dad and Loretta looked at her with concern, but she gave them a hand gesture that everything was okay and stepped out of the room.

He couldn't even get a word in until finally she took a breath and he told her, "Baby, calm down for a second. If you give me a chance to explain, I'll let you know why I wasn't answering. After I finished running around on yesterday, I pulled up to the club and there were two officers waiting outside for me. They said me and Rufus were suspects in Paul's murder." Renae's heart sank to her stomach. She knew sooner or later they were going to figure it out. Ruben went on to tell her they believed he killed him out of revenge and retaliation for Paul shooting him.

"I told them I was not sure who shot me that day, and never reported anything of that sort. Then the detective told me that rumor was that I had killed him, and that with the help of Rufus, we disposed of the body in the Elgin Forest Preserves. They started bringing up my background and how they knew that I used to be big in the streets. I told them rumor was Tupac and Elvis were still alive and were neighbors living in the Catskills but how likely was that. Anyway, they kept us there all night and *just* let us go a few minutes ago."

She was relieved they let him go but now was upset that it took him so long to call her. "If you were out this morning why am I just now hearing from you? I have been worried out of my mind! I told you they were"

He cut her off, "I know, Baby. I didn't want to text you and knew you were in church so I waited until I thought you were out." He hoped she would understand. "What are you doing now? Maybe we can link up for a little while before I go into work this evening, and we can talk about it then."

She knew she was about to say too much so she just kept it moving. "I am getting ready to eat dinner with Ms. Loretta and my daddy. How about I give you a call when we're done?"

"That sounds good. I'll be waiting. Love you, girlfriend."

"Love you too, but I'm still mad. You could've at least sent a quick text." She said before she disconnected the call and walked back into the family room.

"Is everything okay, Baby Girl?" Her dad asked.

"Yes. Everything is fine for now." Ms. Loretta walked in with her dad's plate and told Renae dinner was ready so she could fix her plate. She went to the kitchen praying that the situation with Ruben didn't turn out as horrible as she had played it in her head.

***

Later that evening, Ruben picked her up and they went to Marlon's to grab a drink and talk about the previous night's events. He told her every detail about what happened the night before all of the questions they asked and the accusations they made.

"Baby, I told you something wasn't right. I knew they were going to eventually find out. What are we are going to do now?" She was starting to draw attention from other patrons of the bar as she got worked up.

He assured her there was nothing to worry about, "Baby, calm down. I told you not to worry and I meant it. They cannot tie anything back to me or Rufus. We got everything under control, and I promise you that I'm not gonna leave your fine ass here for nobody else to swoop in and take from me." That brought a bashful smile to her face. She wasn't completely sold on it, but she let it go for now. She'd wait and see how it played out. She did tell him that she wanted to know everything as it happened so she wouldn't have to guess and worry about what was happening. He promised her that he would let her know everything about the development of the case.

Sunshyne

Sunshyne was up early Monday morning cooking breakfast for the kids. She went to bed early the night before. Maia wanted to go to Jump Zone once they left the movies, and she got her wish. Maia never got tired of that place, but her siblings were just glad she was over Chuck E. Cheese. After Jump Zone, they grabbed something to eat and went home. The kids ate and got ready for bed, Sunshyne took the moment to enjoy the peace and quiet. She popped open a bottle of Bartenura Moscato and watched Kevin Hart's stand up special, *Let Me Explain*. She had seen it several times before but cried laughing every time she watched it.

She and Kody had texted while she watched the girls play at Jump Zone. MJ didn't move from the chairs, texting and playing games on his phone. She told Kody she wouldn't be able to make it out, but they made plans to meet up again for lunch today since their shops were closed. Sunshyne was excited to see him again. She just needed to play it cool. She had given herself to Richard so easily and without limitations that she didn't want to make the same mistakes with Kody.

Sunshyne was deep in thought when Maia came in the kitchen, "Mommy, I'm ready to go. Can you tell MJ and Mariah to come on? They are taking too long."

"Why are you in such a hurry to get to school today, young lady?"

"It's Brandon's birthday, and he said his mom was making cupcakes for everybody."

"Well, you do know that Ms. Helen isn't going to let you eat them for breakfast so you might as well eat you some of mommy's delicious pancakes while you wait for your brother and sister." Sunshyne placed four silver dollar pancakes and a couple slices of bacon on a plate in front of Maia.

Maia had a puzzled look on her face and hesitated before taking the plate. "Only four?"

"How many do you need, Little Girl? Your brother and sister gotta eat too."

"They not gon eat. They are spending too much time trying to look good for their friends."

Sunshyne chuckled and shook her head, "Eat what you have, and if you finish those you can have more." She finished cooking.

Ten minutes later Maia finished her pancakes and put her plate in the sink. By the time Sunshyne came out of the room from getting dressed, all three of them were sitting, waiting on the couch.

"Did y'all eat?" Sunshyne asked the older two.

Mariah had eaten a couple pancakes and some bacon. "Naw. I'm just gonna grab something from the cafeteria," MJ responded.

"Okay. Let's go so I can get y'all to school." Mariah and MJ ran ahead to race for the front seat. This time Mariah won because she remembered they parked down the street instead of in the back as she normally did. As soon as they turned off the block, Sunshyne's phone chimed. She opened her message app to see a text from Kody.

Good morning, beautiful. I hope I am not waking you.

She waited until she dropped MJ and Mariah off before she texted him back.

Good morning. Dropping kids off to school. Are we still on for lunch? He texted back immediately.

Of course. I wouldn't pass up an opportunity to see your beautiful face. How is 12:30?

That's fine. I should be by the shop then. I have a few things to take care of there. C ya later.

Alright. See u then.

Sunshyne pulled out of the roundabout beaming with a schoolgirl grin as she drove Maia to school.

Sunshyne

Sunshyne had been at the shop for about an hour unloading the shampoos, conditioners and other hair supplies she received on Saturday when Kody knocked on the window. He was early, yet again. She appreciated his punctuality. She thought he was nothing like Richard who would call and say he was pulling up to the house arriving fifteen minutes later. Never mind that. She didn't want to start comparing him to Richard, and honestly she didn't want to think about him right now either. Kody was handsome standing there in the doorway. His hair was neat and his face smooth and creamy. He had on a pair of Levi 550s, a brown and tan plaid button down, and some tan Timbs. As she was taking him in as she walked to unlock the door, a burst of excitement went through her body. She knew he was going to have her. It was just a matter of when was going to be the right time.

She opened the door, "Good afternoon, sir."

"Good afternoon, sweetheart. You ready to go?"

"Almost. I just have one more box to put away. You are always early, and I am never ready when you get here. I don't like waiting so if you are trying to impress me... it is working."

"Naw not trying to impress you. Well, I guess kinda I am but my dad always told us that it is better to be an hour early than a minute late. So take your time I will put that down in the plus column for me." They both chuckled, and Sunshyne went back to putting the rest of the supplies away. About five minutes later they were on their way out the door.

Kody had chosen a small friendly Caribbean restaurant on the north side. He raved about the food and said it was one of those restaurants that you drive by a million times but would never think to eat at. From the looks of the outside he was right, but once you stepped in the door you could see and smell why he chose it. The rich savory aromas tingled her senses as soon as he opened the door. The walls were bright, colorful and held pictures of well-known Caribbean artists and tropical scenery. The hostess greeted them and showed them to their table. Sunshyne knew exactly what she wanted. She always ordered oxtails, with rice and peas, and plantains whenever she ate at this type of place. Nothing else. Kody ordered the red snapper with cabbage and mac and cheese.

Once the young lady who took their order walked away Kody said, “I’m glad you decided to go on another date with me.”

“Me too. I was a little bummed that things didn’t work out yesterday, but I promised my children a movie. They weren’t ready to go home after the movie, so we just made a complete day of it.”

“Not a problem, Sweetheart. I know how kids get. I mean, I don’t have any of my own yet, but when my nieces and nephews get me out, they make sure they do and get everything they want.”

“No kids, huh?” She responded, kinda surprised.

“You say that like it was shocking.”

“Well, I am a little shocked. A black man as handsome as you are,” she stated plainly, “with no kids at your age is kinda shocking. Do you not want any kids?”

“Yes ma’am, I do want kids. At least a couple. I just haven’t found the right one to have them for me. Actually, I was almost a father a few years back. I had been with someone for a few years. She got pregnant but did not want children at the time and got an abortion without telling me. The only reason I found out was her cousin slipped up and mentioned it. When I asked her about it she simply told me that she wasn't ready for children and it was her decision. She didn't feel she owed my any other explanation. Long story short, I blew up and we didn't last much longer after that."

"I'm sorry to hear that," Sunshyne said with sincere empathy.

"Maybe you will have one for me, or at least let us start working on one." He brought his hand up as if he was shocked those words escaped his mouth. "Oops. Did I say that out loud?"

Just as he let those words slip from his mouth, the server set their plates in front of them. The waitress determined they didn't need anything else so she told them to enjoy their food and walked away. Once she was out of earshot, Koby looked Sunshyne in the eyes, "I hope I didn't offend you, but I'm just gonna put it out there. You are beautiful, and I want to spend as much time as I can with you. I know you have responsibilities so I won't pressure you, but whenever you can fit me in, I would like to see you."

Just then her eyes got big. Kody thought he was moving too fast until he noticed she was staring past him. Before he had the chance to turn around Richard stopped at the table. "Hey, Nette. How are you?"

With no enthusiasm at all in her voice, Sunshyne dryly replied, "Hey. I'm good." There was an awkward pause before Richard introduced the woman he was with as Evelyn. He stood there waiting for Sunshyne to introduce Kody. When he saw that she wasn't he went ahead and introduced himself. He offered his hand toward Kody. "Richard."

Kody extended his hand and was about to reply when Sunshyne interrupted, “My apologies. Richard this is Kody. He just opened up the barber shop acr…”

Richard jumped in before she could complete her sentence, “The one across the street from your shop. What’s the name again? *Correct Cuts*? Yea I meant to bring my nephews there when you opened but my brother ended up bringing them. I’ll have to stop in and check you out one day. I don’t mind supporting when I can.

Richard could see both Sunshyne and the hostess becoming annoyed, so he cut the conversation short. “I won’t hold you from your lunch. Enjoy.” He directed his date to the table where the hostess was standing.

When they were alone again Kody broke the silence, “That was a little weird.”

“Yea. He is my ex. It is weird that he wanted to have a whole conversation and that he just happens to be here, but let’s not talk about him. He is the last thing I want to talk about right now. You had just said some good stuff and I don’t want him to ruin it. If you don’t mind I would really like to get back to where we were before being so rudely interrupted.”

“No problem, Sweetheart. I don’t want anything to spoil our day.”

“Thank you. I think you were telling me how beautiful I was and how you wanted me to have your babies.” They both let out a very animated laugh that caught Richard’s attention. He wasn’t showing it but inside he was seething with disgust.

“Yes. Beautiful you are. I won’t pressure you into having my children quite yet but don’t totally push out getting in some practice,” he said and winked his eye.

Sunshyne blushed, “I’ll keep it in mind.” They finished up their food and conversation before Kody got the attention of their server to ask for the check. Once they got into the car, Kody offered to take her for ice cream. Sunshyne could eat a hot fudge sundae anytime. They found the nearest Baskin Robbins, ate ice cream and chatted. All the while they were driving, Sunshyne had an eerie feeling in the pit of her stomach. This was the second time in just a few days that she felt something was out of place after seeing Richard. She knew it wasn’t a coincidence and wasn’t going brush it off, but for now she would enjoy her time with Kody.

***

After ice cream and a long, very interesting, conversation, Kody dropped Sunshyne back at the shop to her car.

Sunshyne thanked Kody. “I had a wonderful afternoon.”

“Me too. Hopefully we can get together again soon.”

“I’m sure we can arrange something.”

“Well, I’ll be looking forward to it.” Kody said with a distinct cheerfulness in his voice. He waited for her to swing her foot into the car and closed the door. He walked over to the shop smiling like he had just won the gold medal at the Olympics, and to him it felt like he had.

Renae

Renae was at work doing her best to stay busy. She tried not to think about the case with Ruben. He didn't tell her much except not to worry because he had everything under control. She was getting bits and pieces from Tanya, and that seemed promising, but she couldn't help but be worried. Her phone rang as she was walking out of the courthouse and to the parking lot.

She tapped the green answer button on the screen and placed her finger on the speaker button, "Hello."

"Hey, baby. How was your day?" She could hear people clapping in the background and remembered one of his nephews had a baseball game.

"It was a rough one. After you and I talked earlier we got a case from yesterday on a mother who drowned her baby earlier in the day and shot one of her older children when she got home from school. One of her neighbors heard the gunshot while he was walking his dog and called the police. She ended up confessing that she was going to kill her last child and herself once he made it home. Thank God he stopped at a friend's house to get a book that he needed to study for a test."

"Baby, that's horrible. I'm sorry to hear that. Well, hopefully I can help your evening get better. When you get done with your girls, I'll have something special for you."

"That sounds good. I'm not sure how long we're going to be, but I'll call you when I'm on my way."

"Okay. I'll see you later." She could hear him yelling to his nephew that he had made a good catch before she disconnected the call. She smiled. She couldn't wait to see him with his own children.

Renae drove a few more blocks and her phone rang again. She was apprehensive about answering it when she saw who was calling. Tanya was her connection to the investigation. She didn't know what to expect when she answered, still she knew she had to answer.

"Hey girl. What's going on?"

"Nothing much. You know my birthday is on Thursday? I'm going to have something at Rosie's if you and your friends want to stop by." Rosie's was a hole in the wall located on the Chicago side of the Glenmont/Chicago border. Renae had never been in there as long as it had been around. Desiree always teased and told her she thought she was too good.

"I will try to make it. You know Desiree loves that place so we probably will come." She tried to convince Tanya and herself.

"Good. I hope you can make it. We haven't hung out together in a long time."

"I know, right. What else is going on with you?" Renae wanted to see if she had any more information about the investigation without coming out and asking.

It was like Tanya knew what she wanted, "Well girl, Mama calls the police almost every other day. They keep telling her they have a few solid leads but can't give her any information. They said they may be making an arrest shortly and will inform her once they do."

Damn. That was not what she wanted to hear. She needed more information than Tanya had right now but hopefully she could get the news about the arrest from her mother before it happened.

Somebody kept calling Tanya's name in the background, "Alright. I gotta go but I hope you make out on Thursday."

"Alright. I'll talk to you." She had pulled up and sat outside Sunshyne's building to finish her conversation. As she hung up the phone Desiree tapped on her window.

***

Renae didn't stay at Sunshyne's long. Sunshyne was giving Desiree a new color and Renae stopped by to hang out for a minute. She told them about the party Tanya was having for her birthday and encouraged them to come.

"Well you know Desiree won't have a problem. I'll see if Michelle can get out as well. I'll also invite the new owners of the barbershop."

"Cool. I'm sure she won't mind. It will make her feel like she's doing something to have some new faces and not the same deadbeats that normally come to her parties. Well, I'm gonna get outta here so I can spend some time with my man before he has to get to work." She gathered her stuff and told Desiree to send a picture of the finished product when she was done.

By the time she made it home, Ruben was cooking dinner and had a bottle of her favorite wine. He grabbed her and planted a kiss on her soft lips. "I thought I would have everything ready by the time you got home but since you're here I want you to sit and relax for a second." He took off her coat, led her to the couch, and poured her a glass of wine. "I'll be back for you shortly." Ruben reappeared in the bedroom doorway about ten minutes later. He motioned Renae to follow him to their room. She noticed the bathroom was dimly lit and the delicate, sweet scent of her favorite bubble bath drifted through the air. Her heart warmed and her smile lit up her face as they got closer to the bathroom door.

"I told you I had something special for you and this is just the beginning. I have something else for you when you're done with dinner. Take your time in there, but not too long, we don't want dinner to get cold—or me either for that matter." He gave her a mischievous wink and went back to the kitchen.

Renae took advantage of the warm, soothing bubble bath Ruben prepared for her. She sank into the tub, and laid her head back, relieving her mind of all the details from Paul's case and the pictures she saw earlier that day in the office. She had been in there for so long that she felt herself dozing off. She washed up and climbed out of the tub. She didn't want to prolong the rest of her evening any longer.

Ruben walked towards the room as she came out. "I thought maybe you had drowned. I was just on my way in to check on you."

"No need, Boo. I'm here. What is that I smell?" Renae tried to get a peak over the breakfast bar but Ruben playfully admonished her, "Have a seat over there. You'll find out soon enough." He directed her towards the dining room table. Minutes later Ruben appeared with two plates of glazed salmon fillets, twice-baked potatoes, and Brussel sprouts. Renae ate her food like she hadn't eaten all week.

"Slow down, Baby. You can chew your food. You're gonna get what you got coming to you. It's not goin' nowhere."

Renae laughed, "Baby, I didn't get the chance to eat lunch with all that was going on in the office today. I am famished, and if you have another piece of fish, I'll take it."

Ruben brought Renae another piece of salmon, and she devoured it. They finished eating, and Renae volunteered to clear the dishes while Ruben showered. He didn't take no time at all. He was back with Renae before she had barely finished and was on the couch watching TV.

"Now who was in a hurry to get back out here?" Renae joked.

Ruben joined her on the couch. She was watching the latest episode of *Love and Hip Hop Atlanta*, but he wasn't interested in what was on the screen. He didn't care nothing about Rasheeda or Joseline. His focus was on the woman sitting next to him. The television was on but Renae wasn't as interested in the show as it seemed, yet she playfully stopped his advances. Ruben continued to plant kisses on her neck and lips until she finally gave in to return his kisses. Once he knew he had gotten her attention, he guided her body so she was lying back on the couch and unbuttoned her night shirt. His kisses moved south on her body. He tickled her neck with his soft, warm kisses. Renae began to feel her temperature rise between her thighs. Ruben completely unbuttoned her nightshirt. He worked his mouth down the length of her body stopping at her breasts cupping them in his hands gently licking and kissing her nipples. He felt her body tremor in his arms and a slight moan escaped her lips. He ran his hand down her body, tracing her belly button allowing his hand to fall between her legs. He twirled her short curly hairs before easing his fingers inside her. She silently moaned as his fingers entered her. She assisted him as he gently pushed his hand deeper until he reached the spot that weakened her body.

Ruben's erection grew with thoughts of losing himself inside her. He wanted to please the gorgeous woman below him. He wanted her to reach the limit of no return before he penetrated her, but the anticipation of her wetness gripping his dick was becoming too much for him.

She reached inside his sweats, grabbed his dick and whispered in his ear, "Give it to me now. I don't want to wait anymore." Her pussy was hot and begging for him to come get it. It was as if she could hear his thoughts. He took her in his arms and carried her to their room. He laid her on the bed, and as he took off his pants he pulled her beautiful brown frame into him.

"You are so gorgeous. I don't know how it happened, but I am the luckiest man in the world."

Ruben climbed on Renae and stared into her sparkling brown eyes as he eased his manhood between her sweet essence. Renae didn't let him enter all the way. She allowed him to tease her and drive her crazy. She stayed right on the edge, feeling the sensation until she couldn't hold back any longer. Her eyes rolled back into her head, fingers gripping the sheets while her muscles absorbing his shaft. She rolled her hips with rhythmic thrusts until her juices flowed and a wave of heat engulfed his manhood.

"Oh damn, baby. That's gonna make me cum," he whispered in her ear. He slowed down the pace. He wasn't ready just yet. He wanted this to last. He put her in different positions, and Renae welcomed Ruben's intense effort to bring her body the indescribable pleasure she needed. Ruben felt her body grow tense one last time. He begged her to cum together before she erupted she obliged. He stroked her deep, long, and slow until he was ready to explode inside of her. Ruben pumped deep and fast making sure he hit the spot that had his name on it.

"Ooh baby. Here it cums," he moaned. He couldn't wait anymore. He felt her heavenly waterfall rush over him, and that's when his juices filled her sweet box. Their bodies fell limp. They laid for a moment with Renae nestled in his powerful, carved arms until her excitement oozed down her leg. She got the rag for them to clean themselves. Renae came back to the bed and allowed Ruben to relax as she gently wiped their juices from his body.

***

Unfortunately, Ruben had to get ready to leave Renae in order to get to the club tonight. He couldn't stay with her wrapped in his arms. He hated he had to leave, but he knew this wasn't going to be much longer before he was home with her every night. He wasn't sure how he was going to make it happen, but he knew he was going to make something happen. He kissed her goodbye and made sure the house was locked up. Even though she didn't want him to leave, she showered with the feeling that this part of her life was finally right.

Sunshyne

Sunshyne woke to the beginning of a beautiful day. The weather remained abnormally warm. The sun filtered in through her blinds, and a lazy wind brushed against the window. She couldn't waste time getting to the shop as she had a full schedule. On the way to the shop she noticed most of the branches that were bare and wiry weeks ago were now coming to life with bright green leaves.

She got to the shop early and had already done a sew-in, a big chop, and a color. While working on her last client for the morning when Michelle walked in the door. "Hey y'all." Everyone in the shop responded with a hello.

"Hey girl. What you doin' over here?" Sunshyne cautiously asked her hoping she wasn't looking to have anything done to her hair because her book was too full to try to squeeze her in.

"Nothing. Dang. Can't a sista stop by to see her friend and invite her to lunch?"

Sunshyne started laughing, "Of course you can. Especially if that sista is treating."

"I got you. How long you gon be?" Michelle sat in the chair at the booth next to Sunshyne's.

"I need about fifteen minutes, and I'll be ready. I just need to fin..." Before she could complete her sentence, Kody walked in the door and headed straight for Sunshyne.

"Hello, ladies." He never took his eyes off Sunshyne.

The women returned their greetings.

He stood next to Sunshyne, "Good morning, beautiful."

Sunshyne's face grew warm. She wasn't sure why, but she felt a little embarrassed. If the room got any quieter her client would hear her heart pounding in her chest.

"Good morning. How are you?"

"I'm so much better now. What's up with you? It's almost lunch time and I'm sure you need to eat. Do you wanna go grab a bite?"

"Sorry. I can't today. I'm having lunch with my friend." Sunshyne corrected herself. "I mean my best friend. Kody, this is Michelle. Chelle, this is Kody."

They both extended their hand to greet one another. "Hello, Mr. Kody. I've heard some good things about you."

"I'm glad they've been good. I wouldn't want to start out wrong before I even get one foot in the door. I've been told you will be the hardest one for me to win over," he said with a smile.

"As long as you know, you're already ahead of the game." Kody turned his attention back to Sunshyne. "Maybe you can give me a call later. I have some stuff to do around the shop so I will be around."

"Sounds good. I'll call you later."

"I will be waiting. Enjoy your lunch, ladies." Sunshyne didn't take her eyes off him until he was across the street. Her client had to clear her throat to get her attention.

"Ooh sorry. We are almost done, Ms. Simpson."

"No problem, chile. I know how it is when that fella gets your attention. We forget everything else." They let out a little chuckle.

About fifteen minutes later Sunshyne and Michelle were headed to Cheesecake Factory to enjoy some girl time. Michelle and Sunshyne arrived at the restaurant about ten minutes later and were seated right away. Michelle ordered the herb crusted salmon with a double portion of asparagus instead of mashed potatoes, and Sunshyne got the smokehouse BBQ burger, medium well, with no cheese, and sweet potato fries. They both ordered iced tea. The waiter repeated their order and told them he would return shortly with their drinks.

"Girl, Kody *is* very easy on the eyes, and he seems to be respectful."

"Yes. He is *FINE.* He is also very respectful and protective—both him and his brother. They have made it their business to make sure everyone is out of the shop and it is locked up before they leave for the night. If it's late one of the barbers make sure our customers get to their cars safely. I haven't gotten to know him too well, but he seems like everything you want in a man. You know what that usually means."

"Alright now. Don't go sabotaging it before it even gets started. Enjoy it for what it is at the moment. You don't have to start planning your divorce yet. You just met the guy. I think you should take your time with this one. Don't go rushing into it heart first, and you won't be so easy to get hurt. Don't let what Marcus or Richard did corrupt your idea of who Kody is either. If he is too good to be true, let him be. You deserve it."

Sunshyne knew exactly what her friend meant by that. Both Marcus and Richard had made her promises they never intended to keep. She wasn't going to allow them to ruin anything for her in the future, but she couldn't help but to be a little cautious. She sucked her teeth, "Girl, shut up. I know. I know. I'm just saying. That's all. I don't wanna keep dating his ass and then six months from now he pop up with a whole family that he's been keeping a secret over up in Wisconsin. Speaking of whole families, I think Richard is stalking me."

Michelle gave her a puzzled look. She wasn't sure how Sunshyne was able to segue way the two, but she just kept going with it. "Why do you think he is following you?"

"Sunday when I was leaving church he was sitting at the corner. Then yesterday he just so happened to pop up with a date at the same restaurant Kody and I were."

"Like you said, he had a date with him and Sunday he could have just been in the area. I mean Glenmont isn't that big. So maybe they are both coincidences."

"Coincidences my ass!" Sunshyne realized she was loud and looked around to see two old women looking their way. She calmed down a little and brought her voice to an almost whisper, "Girl it ain't no damn coincidence. First of all, when I saw him on Sunday he said he was on his way to Morton Center to see his daughter's recital. If he was, then that meant you were lying to me because you said you and the kids were skating, and I know you ain't lied to me about that. If he had been at a restaurant around here and we bumped into each other then maybe I could have went for it, but we were all the way down on the north side, close to Wrigley Field. So there ain't no way we just happened to be eating at the same place. I know the next time I see his ass I'm gonna ask him so I can see the look on his face. I'll know if he is on something or not."

"Now that you say all that, it does sound a little fishy. Maybe you should say something to Terrell. You know he don't like his ass no way."

"Yea, but I don't want to get him involved unless I necessarily have to cause you know Terrell ain't about to play with him."

"Just be careful. Richard sounds like he is losing it, and I don't need you to come up missing."

The ladies paused on the conversation as the waiter placed their entrees in front of them. Sunshyne asked the waiter to wait so she could cut her burger to ensure it was cooked enough for her. Once she gave her approval he asked if there was anything else they needed and moved on to assist other patrons.

Sunshyne continued the conversation about Richard, "Girl, I think he started going crazy back when I left him alone and Monica's baby turned out to be Paul's."

"They say karma is a mothersomethin and he got hit hard," Michelle commented.

"Yea, but I kinda feel bad for him. I mean I know I shouldn't, and I don't feel bad enough to take his ass back. Still, I can't help it. Anywho enough of his sorry ass. You think Kody is cute, huh?"

They both let out a little laugh. "Yes. He is a nice looking brotha. I just hope he ain't another one of these sorry brothas. You deserve someone who is going to treat you right and be straight up."

"You damn skippy. This time I'm not going to rush into anything. We are going to have fun, get to know each other, and if it turns into something else then so be it. So how is everything on your end?"

"Everything is going good with me. The business is booming. We are thinking about expanding the warehouse soon. Walter says that we don't have enough machines or manpower to keep up with the orders coming in. Carlton and I are doing good—real good. The kids are doing well in school. I think Kay Kay is set on going to Hampton, and I'm going to let her follow her own path. It's not Rhodes but at least it's an HBCU. As much as I want her to attend Rhodes, this is not about me. I thank you for being that voice in my ear to make sure I don't do something I regret. Even though I know I couldn't *make* her choose my alma mater, I'm glad you talked me out of trying to guilt her into going."

"You know I got you. You don't want to be the reason for any regrets she has later on. Oh yea, before I forget, Tanya is having a party at Rosie's for her birthday on Thursday. I know it's a weekday~~,~~ but I may go for a little while. If you wanna go for a couple hours after you get the kids settled, let me know. We don't have to stay long."

Michelle pulled out her phone to check her calendar. "I don't have to be in until late Friday morning~~,~~ but let me see what's going on at the house. I will let you know when I get home tonight. I may even see if Carlton wants to come out. You know he don't really like hanging out; maybe I can talk him in to coming out for a few drinks."

"Cool. I might just invite Kody and his brother so they can get a taste of Glenmont's night life. Not that it's much, but he talks about how he passes by there on his way into the shop and wants to go to see what it's all about. This will be his chance."

The ladies finished their food and went back to work. Michelle dropped Sunshyne off at the shop and went to the warehouse. As soon as Sunshyne walked through the door, Lollie couldn't wait to tell her, "Girl. You got Kody's nose wide open. He has been over to the corner store at least five times. Every time he walks to and from, he is straining his eyes to see if you're in here. Once I thought he was gonna walk into the *no parking* sign for not paying attention to where he was going."

Lollie laughed and Sunshyne hit her on the arm, "Whatever."

Meechie chimed in, "No. She is serious. You got him hooked."

Sunshyne smiled as she walked back to get her next client from under the dryer. It felt good to have someone interested in her and *only* her. At least that's the feeling she got. All she knew is that he gave her butterflies every time he was around.

***

Sunshyne called Kody after her last customer as promised. He invited her out to dinner, but she declined. She wanted to hang out with him but needed to get home to the kids. Maia had a project to finish for school, and Sunshyne promised she would help. She cleaned the shop and got her tools ready for tomorrow. Normally, Meechie was done early during the week. Ever since her mother-in-law took ill, she started earlier than her business partner because she needed to get home to take care of her mother-in-law and relieve her husband. She would open the shop, and Sunshyne would close. This worked for Sunshyne because she could get the kids off to school and still be home early enough to put them to bed. She'd been doing a lot more with all she had been through last year. She promised the kids they would never go through any of that ever again no matter what. Sunshyne had to decline the dinner date. As she double-checked her appointments at the front desk, Kody tapped on the glass door.

She unlocked the door, "Hey there, sir."

"Good evening, sweetheart. Since dinner is a no-go I thought I would get a few minutes with you while you finished here. How was lunch?"

"Lunch was good. Got a chance to catch up a little with my girl. We don't get to hang out too much these days. Seems like we are busier than ever. How was your day?"

"We were busy. I don't know what's going on around here but I haven't cut that many heads or shaved that many faces in a while. I usually sit back and talk ish more than cut hair, but not today. Your baby brother came through and got a cut, said he was going out of town or something."

"Yea. Him and some little chicken head he is dealing with." She rolled her eyes. "I hate we can't have dinner tonight but I gotta get home to help my baby girl with a school project. It's due next week and I don't want to wait until the last minute to get it done."

"That's cool. That just means you owe me a date, and trust me, I will collect on it. We have plenty of time to eat together. Homework comes first. Time with the kiddies is very important because once it's gone then it's gone forever, and I will never be the one to take you away from them. I will never be able to understand how hard it is for a single woman raising children, but I'm sure it's not easy. Maybe we can get together this weekend some time. That will work for me."

"This weekend is good. The kids will be with their father so I will have all the free time in the world. Before I forget, there is a party Thursday at Rosie's. Maybe you and Niko or some of the fellas wanna stop through. It isn't much but you said you'd like to see some of the Glenmont life."

"Sounds cool. That's the place on Howard I had mentioned to you? I don't really care about Glenmont, just one particular lady here. As long as you will be there, I'm there. I wouldn't pass up a chance to spend any kinda time with you."

A hint of red spread across her cheeks as they burned from his charming words. "Alright. Well I better get home. I'm sure I will see you in the morning." She grabbed her purse and headed for the door.

Kody opened the door, waited for her to lock up and walked her to her car. He almost stole a kiss as he opened her car door but didn't want things to become awkward. So he simply offered a, "Have a good evening, young lady." He closed her door once she was safely in her vehicle.

As Sunshyne drove away she watched him through her rear-view mirror thinking about the sermon Pastor Collins liked to preach quite often. She wondered was this man too good to be true. Did he have some dark secret that was going to eventually come out once she got to know him better, or was it time, and her morning was coming? She was so occupied with Kody that she didn't notice Richard's car parked on the adjacent block a couple cars back. He had seen her with this cat one too many times and didn't like it at all.

Renae

It was Thursday and Renae woke up in a good mood. She laid in bed watching Ruben sleep replaying her conversation with Tanya the night before. The Elgin police were still looking for the car that was spotted leaving the forest preserves around the time Paul was killed. They told her mother it may be almost impossible to find it if they ever do. On top of that, there was no real evidence against Rufus and Ruben other than the fact that Paul could have been the one to shoot Ruben. They also told her the case was ongoing despite the fact that Ruben continuously told them he had no idea who shot him. After further investigation, they learned from an informant that Ruben wasn't the only one who had a motive for wanting Paul dead. They also learned that Paul and a couple of his boys robbed a local gambling house a couple weeks before his death, and more than one person *had been looking to do him some serious harm* was the words the police used when talking to his mother. They told her that it might not be as easy as they previously thought. Yet, they assured her they were not going to give up and would keep her informed if they learned something new. Tanya's mom would not let go of the fact that she felt Renae had something to do with it all. For now her mind was at ease. She talked with Desiree a few times over the past couple of days and couldn't wait to hang out with her best friend.

Ruben rolled over, "Good morning, beautiful."

"Good morning, baby. What time did you finally make it in last night or should I say this morning? I didn't hear you in the shower or feel you climb into bed for that matter."

"Yea. I took a shower in the other bathroom so I wouldn't wake you. They let Bruce's party go past closing I have some good news." Ruben's eyes were bright with excitement.

"What is it?"

"You know how I been talking about wanting to take over Lester's shop when he retires? Well, Bruce's brother is the manager of the Chase on Oakton, and we got to talking about some things. To make a long story short, I told him the plans I'm working on; he told me to come holler at him when I'm ready. He's going to help me get a loan as long as I come with a strong business plan and a down payment. Now I gotta get back in school and finish learning the basics."

"Alright now. That's great, baby. I know you got this."

"Yea. I'm tired of working for someone else -- the BS that goes on at the lounge and especially being away from you so many nights. I should have made the move a long time ago, but I was procrastinating. I gotta kick shit into gear."

"Go ahead then. Whatever you need from me, I got your back."

"I know you do, and I appreciate you. Soon enough we won't have to look over our shoulders anymore and I can give you the life you deserve. Late hours at the lounge and leaving you alone throughout the night is not right and you need better. I meant it when I said I want to be the one to give it to you." He grabbed her pulling her on top of him. Renae got ready to speak but before she could utter a word he kissed her gently. She opened her mouth and returned the affection despite the overwhelming aroma of his morning breath. His hands caressed her back and moved down before pulling her closer into him where she could feel he was just as excited as she was. He raised her teddy to see if she had gone to bed with no panties on—just the way he liked it. He became more excited as his fingers played with her secret spot and felt how moist she was. He couldn't wait any more. He flipped her on her back, removed his boxers, and entered her without hesitation. As he lifted her legs she tilted her hips to allow him to go as deep inside of her as he could. She moaned in ecstasy every time his manhood hit the spot that had only his name on it. Her moans grew louder with each thrust. She could no longer contain herself. She screamed with sheer pleasure. A warm wet blanket of her juices covered his entire shaft. As she released the last of her juices, she pushed him off, moved to the edge of the bed, and got on all fours. He knew exactly what to do. She always seemed to position herself in just the right way so that he didn't have to stand on his tip toes nor scrunch down to enter her. He rubbed her ass before bringing her into him. He slid in with ease because by she was dripping wet. With every stroke he watched himself disappear inside of her.

"Give... it... to... me... baby. Don't... stop! Please. Please. Don..."

With every word he stroked harder and faster. He didn't want to but he couldn't hold it any longer. She arched her back and tightened her muscles around him. Her tight, warm pussy made it hard for him not to explode. He grabbed her hips and pulled her all the way back into him. She didn't need much help. She got down on her elbows and threw her body back harder into him until she felt him pulsating, filling her body causing her body to succumb and release her essences with him. They were both spent. They rolled over and laid cuddling until Renae felt their nectars running down her leg. She got up to shower so that she could get to work. Ruben had fallen back to sleep by the time she was done. She kissed him on the forehead before heading out the door.

Sunshyne

Sunshyne was at the shop early this morning. Ms. Taylor had to be in and out in time to make her early afternoon flight. Maia had to be dressed and fed before leaving the house, and MJ was instructed to make sure she got on the bus. When she arrived at the shop, there was a package at her station with a card taped to it. Yesterday Meechie closed the shop and hadn't told her about any package. To her surprise there was a beautiful arrangement of assorted lilies and mini carnations. She opened the card, and the front simply read, *New Beginnings*. Inside it read, *You walked into my world and every day is brighter*, and he added his own sweet short message. *We haven't known each other long, but every morning I wake up wanting to hear your voice or see your face. I don't want to scare you off, but I also don't want this feeling to end*, signed *Ya boy, Kody*. She was impressed because during one of their *get-to-know-you* conversations she mentioned that lilies were her favorite flower, and he remembered. It made it a little more special because he specifically told her that he doesn't retain much but remembered the important stuff. Sunshyne sat in her chair wondering maybe there were real men in the world who valued relationships. She didn't want to put the cart before the horse, but she also wanted their relationship to grow. Ms. Taylor tapped on the glass door before she could get real deep in her thoughts. Smiling, she placed her card at her station next to her flowers and unlocked the door.

"Girl, you awful chipper this morning." By the time she got over to Sunshyne's booth she realized why. "Ohh somebody got flowers, huh?"

"Yes ma'am, and for no reason at all."

"Oh, there's a reason sweetheart. There's always a reason," Ms. Taylor laughed.

Sunshyne just shook her head putting an apron around Ms. Taylor and lead her to the bowl. She hurried to change the subject. "Where are you headed this time?"

"My girlfriends and I are going on a cruise to Jamaica. A couple of us have been once before but it is such a lovely place that I don't mind going again. It is a beautiful island."

"I am sure you will have plenty of fun. I need a vacation myself but can't find time to take one."

"Baby, there is always time, you just got to make it. Don't let too much time get away that you begin to regret not doing anything with it. I promised myself a long time ago I was going to live. Before Earl passed, we lived it up together and now that I'm by myself I..." Ms. Taylor was interrupted by a knock on the door. Sunshyne looked up and it was Kody. A smile as wide as the Grand Canyon covered her face. After Sunshyne massaged the conditioner into Ms. Taylor's hair, she went to open the door. Kody walked in with a box of donuts and two coffees.

He noticed Ms. Taylor at the shampoo area, "I'm sorry ma'am. I only brought this beauty here a coffee. If you'd like I can run and grab you one."

"Naw, sweetheart. I'm ok. I had breakfast at the house, and I have a cup of tea with me."

Kody handed Sunshyne her cup and planted a kiss on her lips before he realized what he was doing. She was a little taken aback but she didn't let him know. She returned the kiss and thanked him for the flowers.

"The flowers are beautiful. Thank you."

"Beautiful flowers for a beautiful lady."

Sunshyne blushed but didn't say anything in response.

After a few seconds of silence, Kody asked where he should put the donuts. She directed him to a countertop near the back of the salon. He came back up to the front. "Ma'am, you have a wonderful day. Ms. Lady, I will see you later. I have a couple meetings, and errands to run so I may not get to see you until tonight."

"That's cool. My book is full anyway and then I gotta get the kids."

"What are you saying woman? That you don't have time for me?"

"I'm telling you don't sweat it, and I'll see you later on tonight. Now get out so I can finish Ms. Taylor's hair before you gotta find her an express flight to meet the cruise ship."

"Alright. Come lock the door behind me." No sooner than he could get it out Meechie came through the door. They spoke their hellos, and he was gone.

"Good morning. How you doing this morning, Ms. Taylor?"

"I'm great. I would be better if this child would come on and get to my hair. Loverboy got her skinnin' and grinnin' so much she can't focus."

Meechie gave a little chuckle. "I see you got your flowers," Meechie said, and gave her a wink.

"Yes. They are beautiful. Thanks for the heads up," she said with a sarcastic tone.

"Girl, I didn't want to ruin the surprise. Plus, I am sure you were much happier walking in to see them at your station than if I had told you."

"You right. Thanks."

The shop began to fill, and Sunshyne got to moving with Ms. Taylor.

Renae

Renae had barely got in her car when her phone started vibrating. She hadn't even had the chance to turn the ringer on after leaving work. Her face lit up when she saw who was calling.

She answered the phone as if she had just won the lottery. "Hey, baby."

"Hey, Girlfriend. How was your day?"

"It was good. How about yours?"

"It's been pretty busy trying to figure out what is needed to get this business up and running. I was hoping we could grab something to eat before you headed out with your girls."

"That sounds good but how about I make us something quick to eat. I'll go take Muffin out and whip up something." Renae had taken some pork chops out the day before that she hadn't cooked. She could fry them and make some rice with broccoli and cheese.

She was just about done cooking by the time Ruben got home. He planted a kiss on his lady's lips. "The house smells good."

"I don't know what you thought. Just because I don't do it often doesn't mean I don't know how to. I have been blessed by the expertise of two great women who could cook."

"I know you can cook. You found the way to my heart and stomach a long time ago." On the way to the fridge he smacked her on her round ass, and Muffin barked.

"That's right. Get him."

Renae took the pork chops out of the pan and fixed their plates. They sat at the small breakfast table and Ruben shared all that he had gathered. He learned that he needed to get back in school. "Robert

Morris has an accelerated business degree program, and if I get everything in order I can start in a few weeks. I already told Donald I won't be working as many nights as I have been. Then I'm sure I'm going to need my beautiful, smart, girlfriend to help me with my studies. You know I haven't touched a book in a long time."

"I told you. Whatever you need. I got you." She was glad he finally figured out something else to do with his life. She realized he had been out of the game for a while but working as a bouncer at the club was not going to provide any type of retirement benefits.

"I figured I would get the business part out the way *first* since I already know a lot about the business itself. I will need to take some technical classes to catch up with what has been happening in the industry lately. I don't think it will take me long to learn it. I was also thinking maybe you might want to figure out what we need to keep the books straight. We can't just have anybody running our money." He looked at her in a way to will her into agreeing to take it on.

"When I said I got you, that's exactly what I meant. We are partners in this. I will look into it. You just focus on what you gotta do." They finished dinner and hung out for a little while longer before Ruben had to leave. He needed to stop by his parents' house before going to the lounge. After Ruben left, Renae loaded the dishwasher and texted Desiree to see what time they were leaving. She settled in her arm chair to relax until she needed to get ready. She thought about the conversations she had with Ruben. She wasn't sure if it was the devil in her head trying to ruin her happiness or God sending her a warning. She took a minute to talk to Him.

"Lord, I know you've been with me through it all. Even when I didn't realize you were there. You know what I've been through, and what it has done to me. I am trying not to hold onto those feelings and insecurities, but I feel them creeping back up. Father, I am still not sure if it is you telling me that my life is going in the direction it should or me willing myself to believe it because I am in love with Ruben. I heard you when you told me my relationship with Paul was toxic, and I didn't listen. Why can't I trust what you are telling me now? Help me Lord. I am listening and looking for everything you say. Help me to recognize your voice in all that I do. I want everything you want for me no matter if it is what I think is best for me or not. In your son's name. Amen."

She laid there for a while hoping God would talk to her but she got a lot of different answers and still wasn't sure what she was hearing. She decided she would talk to Pastor Collins. Maybe he could help her get some type of understanding.

Sunshyne

There weren't a lot of people in the place when Michelle and Sunshyne walked in but that was the plan. Get in and out before it gets full and a lot of the regular crowd showed up. Of course, there were no signs of Renae and Desiree yet. It was still early so they decided not to trip just yet. They greeted the guest of honor, wished her a happy birthday and ordered a drink. They got ready to pull out their money when Ricky, a guy they went to school with, offered to pay. They caught up with him on old times while they waited on their drinks. The place began to get crowded, and Ricky had gone back to hanging with his boys. All of sudden Sunshyne felt somebody on her back and arms around her waist. She knew exactly who it was after catching a whiff of his cologne.

She turned to face him, "Hey there." She looked immediately behind him and saw Niko standing there like he was security. "Hey Niko."

"Hey, Jeanette."

She introduced Michelle to Niko and turned back to Kody. "You're lucky I knew your cologne because you almost caught a right hook."

"Thank God for the little things." He gave her a peck on the lips.

"Would you ladies like another round?" Niko asked.

Sunshyne didn't hesitate to tell him what she was drinking but Michelle declined. Michelle noticed Desiree and Renae walking in so she waved them over to bar. They went to speak to Paco before coming over. People were already drunk, and the party was just getting started. This is why she wasn't staying long, Michelle thought. About an hour into it,

Michelle was ready to go but she could tell Sunshyne was enjoying herself. She had an early morning so she asked Sunshyne if she could get a ride home.

"Girl, go ahead. I'll get a ride home." She asked Niko to make sure Michelle got to her car and told Michelle to text her when she made it home.

The DJ finally played music Sunshyne wanted to dance to. She tried to pull Kody out onto the makeshift dance floor, but he was not having it. Instead she danced in front of him at the bar. She whined and rolled her hips to the melodic sound of *Murder She Wrote*, while Kody enjoyed every sensual moment. It made him wonder even more what their first time of making love would be like. If she moved like this on the dance floor, he could only imagine what it would be like with a *private dance*. They listened to a little more music, then Sunshyne told Kody she was ready to leave. He was ready to go as well. He had seen a few fellas that had been coming to get their hair cut, but, for the most part, he didn't know too many people in the place.

Sunshyne walked over to Desiree while Kody and Niko had gone to get the car, "I'm heading out now. I'll call you tomorrow but let me know when you make it in please."

"Alright, but contrary to popular belief you are not my mama, and I am a big girl."

"Ok. Just make sure I get a text or phone call. Talk to you tomorrow." They hugged and she left. On the way out she almost didn't see Richard in the corner and she definitely did not notice him fuming as he watched her move all over Kody. She saw the weird look on his face, and immediately felt a knot in her stomach. That nervous feeling stayed with her the entire ride home. Kody dropped his brother to his car at the shop and took Sunshyne home. Sunshyne jumped out the car as soon as they pulled in front of her house.

He walked her to the door and leaned in to kiss her good night but noticed the distressful look in her eyes. “Are you alright, Sweetheart? You were quiet the whole ride home.”

She looked him straight in his eyes and tried to hide her worry the best she could. “I’m ok. Just a little tired. Thanks for asking though.” They kissed, and she went in the house knowing full well that everything was not okay. She had known Richard too long to know he was on something. Kody felt there was something more to it but didn’t want to push anymore. Kody knew that one day she was going to trust him enough to share it all with him.

Renae

Renae got to see Pastor Collins. She told him her dilemma and uncertainty regarding the clarity of God's voice. He gave her words of encouragement.

"Don't be confused," he told her. "The first voice you hear whether you feel it's good or bad is Him. Don't worry about the sound of the voice, it's the content. He doesn't speak to us all the same, and we that know Him will know when He is speaking. A lot of times we have been comfortable living in the mess that we've been in that we get scared to enjoy some normalcy in our lives." He went on to tell her, "Be happy. Don't live in fear. The enemy will always do what is necessary to keep you miserable, but God comes to give you life, and bless you more than you even want to be blessed."

The confirmation was there. She was going to enjoy what she had with Ruben and stop thinking of ways to destroy it. If she was going to pray for guidance then she needed to heed what she heard in response and not allow her doubts to take over. She had resolved that she would have to believe what God was saying was best for her no matter if she could see it or not. More importantly she knew she had to continue to strengthen her relationship with God. She wanted to be able to discern his voice and not have to run to Pastor Collins for clarity every time she was uncertain.

As she sat replaying the conversation over and over in her head, she got a text from Ruben.

Hey Sweetheart. Thinking about you. Don't make any plans for tomorrow. See you later.

Hey my luv. Alright. What's going on?

Sis decided she wanted to do more for Mom's bday. I'll tell you more about it later.

Ruben was celebrating his mother's birthday with his family. She wasn't sure what else they had planned. She was glad they were going to do something else because she hated missing the dinner. Her dad and Ms. Loretta needed help with some stuff today. She had tried to push it until tomorrow after church, but they insisted on today. After she finished with Ms. Loretta and her dad she decided to go home and chill. She ended up watching a *NCIS* marathon until she fell asleep. She woke up to Muffin barking at Ruben.

"Hey girl. You been sleeping all day?"

She looked at the clock realizing she had slept for hours. "It looks like I have. I must have been tired. How did everything go? Was she excited?"

"You know how she was. She tries to play it cool, but she was very happy."

"I hope you told her I wanted to be there. I could have because what I did for my parents didn't take all day." She didn't give him a chance to tell her what he was texting about earlier. "What's up for tomorrow?"

"Kim decided she wanted to have something at her house for Mom's birthday. She had been talking to some of the ladies at her church and in her little social club. I came in at the end of the planning. They felt since my mom had done so much at the church and in the community, they would have something to honor her 75th birthday. Collectively, it was decided to have a meet and greet type of party. We're going to serve finger foods and appetizers, and people can come by to give their well wishes."

"That sounds nice. I'll call Kim and see if she needs help with anything. I'll also let Dougie and Desiree know. They had her in sixth and seventh grade. Maybe they can get on Facebook and let her other students know. I am sure they would love to stop by. I was always jealous of the way they spoke about her. I, unfortunately had Ms. Bakalar and Mr. Ellis."

"That sounds like a plan. I'm sure she would be surprised by her former students. I think Kim has everything she needs but you can give her a call. I ran into Desiree at the gas station after leaving dinner, and she said she was gonna call you. Maybe your dad and Ms. Loretta may stop by. I know what we're serving won't touch her Sunday dinner but I'm sure they will enjoy themselves."

"I will let them know. They said they would attend church with me tomorrow. I will ride with them if they don't have anything planned."

"Nice. You may have a full house with you tomorrow. I was gonna try to go to service tomorrow as well. I haven't been to anybody's church in a long time, and I know you've been wanting me to come with you. I think tomorrow would be a better day than any."

Renae's heart fluttered. This was the one thing he hadn't done that she really wanted him to do. She wasn't going to push him. She waited until he was ready. She knew one day God would place it in his heart to do so, and now here he was willing to come to New Light with her.

"Are you serious?! Ok. I will let them know we are going to the second service. That will give you time to get a few hours of sleep after work tonight," she was so excited she could barely get the words out. She looked up at him and pressed her lips to his, "Thank you."

"For what?"

"For just being you."

"Baby, I love you. I just want you to be happy. You've had enough bullshit to deal with in your life, and some even added from me, but all that is behind us now. Life for us is about to be sweet. You are my baby. Now let me get ready to get up outta here before all this lovey dovey stuff makes me wanna do something to you before I gotta be at the club."

"Would that be a bad thing?"

"See. I knew you only wanted me to be your boy toy."

"Bye, Ruben. Get ready for work. I'm going to go call Dee. She must have called about tomorrow while I was sleep."

Renae took Muffin for a walk and called her friend while she was out. After their hellos, Desiree asked her for an update on the investigation. Renae filled her in on what she learned so far, and how Ruben and Rufus had been picked up.

"Dang. You ain't told a sista nothing." She playfully reprimanded her friend.

"Girl. I really didn't want to say anything until we got more information from Tanya. I wish they would just forget about his sorry ass, but I know his mama is hurting and won't let them give up so easy. I just pray that it's all over sooner rather than later."

"LOL. How you gon cuss and then talk about praying all in the same sentence?"

"I'm still a work in progress. I normally would have said… never mind." They both laughed. "Will you be at Ms. Bradshaw's party tomorrow? I think it should be nice. I just hope it's a good turnout since they started planning last minute. Oh shoot, let me text Dougie and tell him about it before I forget." She texted her brother the details. As soon as she got off the phone with Desiree, she would call Dougie.

"I think tomorrow will be fabulous. So many of her students still talk about her to this day. I'm sure there will be a good turnout. She has done so much in the community with everyone's children."

"Yea, you're right. It is going to be great. Speaking of great, guess who will be at church tomorrow?" Renae responded before she had the chance to open her mouth. "Daddy and Ms. Loretta, *annnddd* Ruben."

"Girl. Shut the front door. How did you finally get him to come to church?"

"I don't know what happened. He just told me that he finally decided he needed to be back in church, and tomorrow was the day. We shall see."

"What do you mean '*we shall see*'? Has he ever said he was going to do something and didn't?" Desiree knew where her friend was going with her tone and wanted to stop her in her tracks before she got started.

"Naw, he hasn't but you know they always say the things you want to hear."

"Girl stop. Stop it right now. Ruben has never been that guy. You told me you weren't going to compare him to anybody else but here you go. Wait until he doesn't show up before you start in on him. I think he might just surprise you."

She replied in a whining voice, "Okayyy. He said he was coming, and I won't write it off just yet."

"Good. Now I gotta get my beauty sleep because if Ruben is coming to church tomorrow, I definitely need to be in the house of the Lord to witness it."

They both laughed. “Alright, girl. I will see you tomorrow.”

Renae called Dougie right away after she hung up so she didn’t forget. He said he would post it everywhere and that he would see her there. She showered and went to bed feeling both hopeful and doubtful about tomorrow not knowing that tomorrow was going to be greater than she had ever imagined.

Sunshyne

Sunshyne woke up early Sunday morning. She had plenty of rest since she didn't go out the night before. This weekend her house had turned into a daycare. Damon's kids called to spend the night. Michelle called to see if Bryson and Chloe could spend the night because they were going out and so was Kay Kay. They did not want to leave the younger ones with Jason. Sunshyne took her younger two and sent MJ and Damon's older two to Jason's. When Kay found out they were coming, she decided to stay in. Sunshyne convinced her that she still wanted the little ones to come over. She ordered pizza, they watched movies and fell asleep in the living room where ever they could find a spot. Now it was time to get everybody moving for church. Damon and Lauren didn't attend New Light. They went to another church across town that started much earlier.

Damon and Lauren picked up the kids, and about another hour or so later Sunshyne and the rest of the children were out the door. Of course, she was running late, and had to park a block away. She hurried the kids into the church so she could get in as much of the service as possible. The deacons were in the middle of devotion; she hadn't missed as much as she thought. Michelle's younger ones spotted her instantly and hurried over to her and Carlton. By the time she sat in the pew behind them, she noticed Renae and her parents. After taking another look, she saw Ruben, Desiree, and Jerome sitting there as well.

She knew Carlton hated talking in church but couldn't help it. She tapped Michelle on the shoulder and leaned forward, "Do you see what I see over there?"

"If you're talking about Ruben, then yes I see him."

"Looks like Nae is going to make an honest man out of him yet." She told Desiree. Before she could get it out, Carlton interrupted, "I am sure whatever y'all are talking about can wait until we get out of church."

Sunshyne knew it was coming sooner or later. "Okay. Okay." She sat back like a scolded child. The deacons turned the service back over to the pulpit for fellowship, and Carlton took the kids downstairs for children's church after fellowship ended. After she made her rounds, Sunshyne took the chance to share the rest of the story with her best friend. She told her about Ruben going back to school and wanting to open his own business. She stopped in her tracks when she heard the musicians begin playing *Chasing after You* for the worship team to sing. The church was a little empty, but you would have never known. The sounds from the congregation were resounding. The choir sang two songs before Pastor Collins got up to preach.

"Just lean over and tell somebody, there is power in the name of Jesus and if they give you a strange look, turn to somebody else. I need a few witnesses that have called on His name and the power has manifested in your life. Go on and testify. Give God the praise."

He asked the congregation to turn their Bibles to James chapter two verses twelve and thirteen. "*It says, 'In everything you say and do remember you will be judged by the law that makes people free. So you must show mercy to others or God will not show mercy to you when He judges you. But the person who shows mercy can stand without fear at the judgement. Turn to your neighbor and tell them, Have mercy."*

"If it looks like they are not trying to hear you, turn to your other neighbor and tell them." After he prayed, he began preaching.

"My desire for us all is that we learn how to treat each other, and that we operate with the heart of God. Here's what we do and how we handle folks. So many of us want to punish people with the law of God but handle them with the heart of man. Oftentimes we convict others by God's law but then we treat them funny with man's heart. He wants you to treat one another the way He treats you with His heart; you should handle each other in the same manner He handles you. As you celebrate God's goodness and all that He is doing in our life, despite the way we treat Him, we should also let that same goodness from us flow to somebody else. Y'all not gon help me preach but I know I'm right when I say it, and according to Ezekiel 11:19-20 in the New Century Version, the Word of the Lord says, 'I will give them a desire to respect me completely, and I will put inside them a new way of thinking. I will take out the stubborn heart of stone from their bodies, and I will give them an obedient heart of flesh. Then they will live by my rules and obey my laws and keep them. They will be my people, and I will be their God. Here is what God says. Your heart is so corrupt that you don't know how to treat one another because you're using the heart of man. Say amen right there. We come to church and thank God for His grace and mercy in our lives but as soon as we walk out those doors we want to treat everyone who has wronged us with a heart of stone. That's where anger and fear come from. That's where getting even with other people comes from."

Renae hoped Ruben got the message. She knew he wasn't the same person he was before, but in case his pride got the best of him again she wanted him to think back to this day. She hoped he'd come back to get several other messages to reinforce what he is hearing this morning.

"Not only do we practice that in the world, but we do it in the church. We need instructions on how to treat people while we are here, and if you read the Bible you will see that your relationship with God is revealed through the relationship with other people. Jesus comes to give us examples of how to do things, and today he shows us how to treat one another. Since we talked about grace at our earlier service, it is only fitting that we talk about mercy this afternoon. You know we will run around this church and kick over chairs for God's mercy. Mercy is God saying, 'You deserve this, but I won't give it to you.' He says, 'I ought to do this, but I am not going to handle you the way you need to be handled.' And I don't know about you, but I thank God He has spared me. I thank God for mercy."

The congregation erupted with shouts and claps. You could hear several *amens* and *Preach Collins* throughout the church. Desiree replayed her life in her head. She reflected on the numerous times she was the recipient of His undeserved mercy. The more Pastor Collins preached, the more she thought about the reoccurring nightmares with Billie as the guest star. Her ex had put her through more than any one person deserved, but God gave her the strength to get out. He spared her for something bigger, and if He could show her mercy she had to give the same to Billie.

Pastor Collins continued with his sermon to encourage the church to show mercy to one another.

He covered the points he wanted them to walk away with. He reminded them that James prompts us that nobody in the church can look down on anyone else. "*We want to limit the severity of the sins we commit, but when it comes to what others do we want to judge them more harshly and say they deserve to go to hell. No matter what your sin is the Bible clearly tells us that the wages of sin is death. James calls that out very clearly. No one can look down on another because we are all sinners."*

"*Y'all don't want to preach with me right there but that's okay. I'll do it by myself because I know I have no business being here today and the only reason I am is because of his mercy."*

"No one can cast anyone into damnation because we all have some kind of issue going on. The only reason we are here is because God has shown us His mercy, and because He has been merciful to us we need to show that same mercy to others."

Pastor Collins continued preaching for a short while longer before he called the deacons and opened the doors of the church. He told them that freedom is the beginning of mercy, they should give it freely. He told them that God wants us to operate in faith despite how they are treated. They should not let the enemy change who they are and continue to trust that the Lord is still in control. He encouraged that when they act freely in mercy and operate in faith, they will be in fellowship with God. Being in fellowship with God will have you treating others the way He does because you will have a heart like God. They will know who people are—good or bad and will show them mercy as He shows us. When the choir was almost done singing Every Praise, Ruben grabbed

Renae's hand to walk to the front with him. He had decided to reconnect with the church.

Sunshyne nudged Michelle in the back. "She is surely making an honest man out of him." Desiree clapped and looked at Jerome with a look of excitement.

Another young lady had also decided to join the church. Once the church clerk was done taking her information she moved onto Ruben. Renae stood behind him rubbing his shoulders with tears flowing from her eyes. One of the nurses brought her some tissue and stood behind her. Minister Lyons took the mic from the clerk and welcomed them both to the church and let them know that once they receive the right hand of fellowship they will be able to receive all rights and privileges of the church. Ruben saw the church standing on their feet, and when he looked to the side he saw Michelle, Desiree, and Sunshyne standing there. They hugged him as he walked back to his seat.

Once church was over, Michelle and Sunshyne stood outside talking to Pastor Collins. They waited on the others to come out of the church while Carlton went to get the car.

Pastor Collins was the first one to speak on Ruben joining the church. "Looks like Renae's boo is tired of being a thug out there in the world."

The two of them knew that there was no telling what might come out of his mouth.

"What is wrong with you? Why would you say something about him like that? That man is not a thug."

"You're right. I think. I'm happy for her though. I hear what's going on, and y'all know I can tell a real "G" when I see one." He imitated someone throwing up gang signs, and they all laughed. The ladies couldn't do anything but shake their heads at him.

"Seriously though, I hear she is happier than she has ever been in a while. She couldn't get that last fella to come to church but brother man decided he wanted to join on his first visit."

More people started filing out of the church, and eventually the others made it outside as well.

Michelle and Sunshyne immediately started ragging on Ruben after they greeted Renae's dad and Ms. Loretta.

"Good job, Ruben," Michelle said.

"Yes. Renae must be the one for you. I haven't seen you in church since... Dang! I can't remember the last time I've seen you in church."

"Whatever Nette. You are going to start seeing a lot more of me here now."

Pastor Collins interrupted, "Congratulations to you again, brotha. We need more men active in the church. I'm not gonna overload you now but I hope you will look into the ministries and see where you fit."

"I definitely will, Pastor. I have heard so many good things about New Light and can't wait to see where I fit in."

They shook hands, and then he turned to Renae, "I'ma go grab the car. Church ran a little longer than expected, and I got a few more errands to run for my mom's party."

"I can go home with Daddy and Ms. Loretta, and ride with them later," Renae said giving him an easy out.

"Thanks, Baby." He gave her a quick peck on the lips, "I'll see you in a little while."

The girls waited for Ruben to get out of earshot and congratulated Renae. This was not only a big day for Ruben, but they knew how hard she tried to get Paul to come to church with her.

"Looks like you are getting Mr. Bradshaw on track. He joined church, and I hear he is getting back in school. You must be giving him," Sunshyne looked over at Renae's dad and Ms. Loretta, and caught her words, "some good advice these days." Her face became warm and flush.

Renae jumped in real quick, "Yea. He's been working to get in school, and he is also trying to take over Lester's shop. I told him I don't know too much about bookkeeping and accounting but I'm going to try to help him as best I can."

Her daddy encouraged her, "Baby, you are a smart girl. I'm sure you will figure out whatever needs to be done."

Michelle told her, "I can help you as well. I know all about that stuff. Whenever y'all get ready give me a call. Well, my chariot awaits. I will see you all in a little while."

Everyone took that moment to say goodbye and made their departures. Renae smiled as she walked to the car. Church was awesome. The choir sang their hearts out. Of course, Pastor Collins preached like nobody's business, and the more she thought about Ruben joining church, her smile grew and her cheeks became plumper with every thought. She was excited at his new commitment and prayed it would last. She could not imagine the day getting any better.

Renae

After church Sunshyne and the kids stopped by to see her parents. The kids weren't there long before Marcus came to get them. They were going to spend time with him since he didn't have much going on this week. She was a little excited. She and Kody made plans to hang out after Mrs. Bradshaw's celebration. She wasn't sure what he had planned but he told her to keep an appetite. She was also instructed not to dress too fancy, but to dress comfortable. Since she was hanging with Kody, she figured she would wait for her parents to get ready and ride with them to the party. She would leave her car at their house.

The room was filled by the time they arrived. They went over to greet Ruben's mom. You could look at her and tell she was something else in her youth. Her face was smooth like melted caramel. There was not a strand of hair out of place, and her makeup was impeccable. She almost looked as she did when she was teaching.

"Hey Shirley," the ladies hugged. Sunshyne's parents wished her a happy birthday. The ladies had a short conversation, and Mrs. Bradshaw told her she needed to come back to the Bid Whist Club. Barbara promised she would real soon. They chatted a little longer before allowing the other guests who arrived to get their chance to visit with the birthday girl. As others left, the room continued to fill with newcomers giving the guest of honor her well wishes. Kody texted Sunshyne so she stepped outside to give him a call.

Hey Sweetie. I know you are with your family and friends so I figured I'd text instead of calling. Hope you all are enjoying yourselves.

"Hey there. It is a huge turnout. I don't know anyone who could have a mean word to say about her."

"That's cool. I was hoping I could swing through in a couple hours and scoop you up. I think you will enjoy what I have planned," he said with a hint of excitement in his voice.

"Sure. That sounds good. If it's alright with you I'll text you if I'm ready to cut out a little earlier."

"That's fine with me. Hell, I'm ready to come get you now but I guess I can wait."

Sunshyne started beaming, "Just a little while longer. I'll talk to you in a little while either way."

They said their good-byes and hung up. As she hung up. Desiree rushed through the walkway. Her steps were hard and fast. Her jaws were tight, and her face was filled with annoyance. She almost walked past Sunshyne, unintentionally, without a word.

"Hey. You just gonna walk past me like I'm not here? What is wrong with you anyway?" Sunshyne wondered if they would ever be able to have a moment in their life that was not filled with any drama, but she knew today was not gonna be that time.

"Sorry, sis. I'm running late. I'll tell you all about it later. I got to get inside. I know Ruben is about to blow a gasket." Desiree grabbed hold of her sister and dragged her along as she talked.

"Hold on. Let's talk about it for a minute before you go inside." Sunshyne raced to keep up with her little sister.

"I don't have time. I have to get inside. I was supposed to bring Ruben something and I know he is wondering where I am." Ruben had been texting and calling Desiree for the last forty-five minutes with no response, but she couldn't. She had too much on her mind and was focused on how she was going to handle the matter at hand.

***

Ruben stood with a couple of his boys when Desiree finally made it to the dining room. She stopped in the guest bathroom before going inside to get herself together. Ruben hurried over to Desiree before Renae came inside from talking to Dougie and a few people they grew up with.

"Where have you been? I been blowing your phone up," Ruben said pulling her into the front room.

"I know, and I'm sorry. I just got a lot of shit going on today so I couldn't respond, but I'm here now. So let's get the show on the road."

Ruben didn't have time to dwell on where she was and why she wasn't answering. He just needed to take care of this now before it got any later. He needed certain people to be around when he did it. He had a couple of his boys gather everyone into the sitting room with his mother. Once he saw everyone in the room that needed to be there, of course his sister would be the last one, he started his speech.

"Y'all know I'm not one for many words so this won't be long. Most of you know how special this lady is to me. She is strong, courageous, and beautiful, both inside and out. She has been through so much but has still seemed to always make it out on top." The room was full of smiles with all eyes on Mrs. Bradshaw as he made his heartfelt proclamation.

When he turned his full attention to Renae, her eyes got wide. He went down on one knee, and her eyes began to fill with joyful tears. The tears that fell from her eyes in the past were insignificant at this point. Those were tears of hurt and pain. These tears were foreign to her eyes. She looked to her dad and then to Desiree. Both gave her a reassuring nod before returning her attention back to Ruben.

"Renae, I know it's only been a short time, but because of you I have been inspired to want more for myself in life. I've been wanting to run my own business for a while, but you gave me a reason to become more serious. I know that whether I'm with you for eight months or eighty years you are the one I want to start a life with you and give you the life you deserve. You are my best friend, and now I want you to be my wife and the mother of my children. I love you and want to spend the rest of my life with you." Ruben's palms had become clammy, and his voice was beginning to crack; he was on the verge of crying.

Tears were streaming down Renae's face. Her right hand was cupped over her mouth attempting to hide the shock consuming her entire body, but Ruben could see she was smiling through her eyes.

Ruben kept it together and got those famous words out before his emotions completely choked him up, "Renae Lynette Cooper, will you marry me?"

She did not hesitate one second, "Yes! Of course I will." Desiree made it across the room and was standing right by her side. After Renae was done giving Ruben and the entire room a glimpse of how much she loved him, she turned to her friend and embraced her. The rest of the room followed either the women giving Renae their well wishes or the fellas joking with Ruben on how he just gave up the best time of his life. He was sure to tell them that he was just beginning that part of his life. Renae felt like she was on cloud nine. Ruben had made her happy from the day they met. She had prayed about their relationship and asked God to tell her what it is He had for her. She decided she would accept this day as the answer to her doubts. Ruben joined New Light and decided he wanted her to be his wife. She was going to let go of expecting the disorder she was *used* to and accept what was happening in her life.

***

Desiree was excited for her best friend. She was doing her best to hide her worries. She deserved every bit of happiness she was experiencing.

"Girl. I am so excited for you. We are going to have the time of our lives planning this wedding. I was told that whatever you want, you get."

Renae gave her friend the side eye, "How long did you know? You're supposed to be my girl. You should have told me."

Desiree laughed, "I've known for a couple weeks but I wasn't gonna tell you. I have been waiting a long time to see this type of smile on your face. Let me tell you again, I am ecstatic for you right now but I gotta get outta here and take care of some stuff. I will call you tomorrow. Enjoy your night." She hugged Renae and told her how happy she was for her and went to say her goodbyes to the rest of her family.

Sunshyne wasn't going to let her get away that easy. She had to give her more details than the little bit she shared earlier. She pulled Desiree away from her parents.

"Ok. Now that all that is over, what's going on with you?" She needed to know details, not the abbreviated version she got earlier.

"I think the ghost of misery past has resurfaced." She kept it cool for her sister's sake. She didn't want her to worry and get everyone else worked up, but she was trembling with rage right now.

"Are you talking about Billie? What the hell? Why do you think so?" You could hear the anger in her voice.

"Yea, that's the one. You know how much I wanted to keep his ass buried and forgotten. When I got home after church there were flowers for me at the security desk. I know it was him because there was a bouquet of fourteen roses. He always gave me fourteen. He would say some bullshit like he didn't give a dozen because it was cliché and thirteen was unlucky." She rolled her eyes thinking about the corny stuff he made up.

"What are you going to do now? Have you told Jerome yet? Did your security see him?" Sunshyne hit her sister with a few more questions before Desiree could stop her.

"Charlie said a delivery service brought them. No, I haven't told him yet, and I'm not sure if I am going to tell him just yet. I haven't had time to think about it. I will let you know as soon as I figure it out but don't worry. You will know as soon as I do." They hugged, and Desiree left to go handle her business uncertain of why Billie had decided to come back around and what he had planned.

Sunshyne

Sunshyne was worried for her sister. She knew Desiree had gotten stronger over the years, but she also remembered how she was when she finally left Billie alone. She didn't trust him as far as she could throw him. For now, she trusted that her sister had everything under control. As much as she promised she wouldn't say anything, she knew that was a lie if she felt things were getting out of control.

She called Kody to tell him she would be ready soon. "Hey, sir. I will be ready in about the next fifteen minutes. I just need to say goodbye to everyone. Yes. Just call when you're in front, and I'll come outside. See you soon."

Sunshyne ran into Michelle as soon as she went back inside. "Looks like Ruben's gonna make an honest woman out of Renae too," Michelle blurted out like she was waiting to see Sunshyne so she could say it to her.

"Ha. It looks that way, doesn't it?" They were happy for the both of them and they thought they made a great couple.

"Me and Carlton are about to get up out of here. I told Kay we wouldn't be here long, and Carlton needs to get home to work on this brief that is due tomorrow."

"No problem. I'm bout to get out of here soon too. Kody is on his way to come get me." Sunshyne's face was beaming.

"You seem to be pretty happy yourself. Looks like everybody is happy and in love, or at least loving the relationships they're in these days. By the way, what was up with you and Richard?"

Sunshyne remembered the encounter she had with Richard earlier. It was right in the middle of

Ruben's proposal. She couldn't understand why he had to push up on her at that time, if at all. He knew they were done but he just wouldn't stop trying. She was still cordial whenever she saw him or he called, but she continued to reject his advances. She was more suspicious of him now that she was beginning to believe he was stalking her. He tried again today. She replayed the confrontation with Michelle.

"What's up Ms. Morris? How are you?"

"Hey, Mr. Franklin. I'm good. How about you?" Sunshyne was rolling her eyes in her head. She just wanted him to say what he was gonna say so they could move on.

"I'm cool, just missing you. I wish you would just give us one more chance. You could have fought harder for us. I know you believe I was lying to you but I meant it when I told you I was leaving her."

"Get the fuck outta here with that," Sunshyne's voice raised and her hands clenched tight. She brought it down to a low whisper. *"You damn right I didn't believe your sorry ass because right after you tried to sell me that dream, you told me your wife was pregnant. So miss me with all your crap. Be for real. The only reason you left her was because you found out the baby wasn't yours."*

Richard tried to interrupt her to get a word in, but she didn't give him an opening. *"After all the waiting and the bull you fed me I can't believe you want to put this on me. Fought harder? You know yourself that sounds crazy. Let me say this and hopefully you will understand loud and clear."* She tried to at least maintain a friendship with him. They had been through too much together but she knew, now, that she had to leave him where he was. He may have realized this because a horrified look came over his face but she continued.

"This will be the last time we have any type of conversation. I tried to remain friendly with you, but you continue to be selfish. From this day forward don't call me, don't text me, and if you see me around act like you don't know me."

"Wow. It's like that? Ol' boy must be treating that cat right—I mean treating you right."

"Fuck you Richard." Sunshyne turned to walk away.

Richard grabbed her arm, "I'm sorry, Nette. I shouldn't have said that."

"You're right. You shouldn't have." She snatched away from him and finished with, *"By the way, he treats me very well.* Then she turned and left him standing there by himself. She heard him calling but refused to turn around.

"I hope you're finally done with this ninja. He makes my ass hurt. Acting as if you were the one who ruined the relationship. It wasn't enough you were putting your life on hold for him, but then the bastard kept giving you false hope." Michelle noticed the look in her friend's face. "Ok, girl. I am done talking about his sorry ass. What's up with Mr. Kody? You gave him some yet? Why didn't you say anything to him about following you or popping up everywhere you were?"

"First of all, I started to say something, but I know he would just deny it. And no, I haven't given him any yet. I think it's gonna happen soon though. I wanted to wait because I want things to be different. Why can't I have both? He isn't like the rest of them so I can't treat this relationship like the rest either. I don't think that's gonna taint our relationship so whenever the time is right I'm gonna just let it happen."

"Good for you. I'm sure I would have given him some a long time ago. I don't have time to be waiting on no *politically correct* timeframe," as she used her fingers to make air quotes. "If you wanna give the man some, go on ahead. That's your." Michelle couldn't finish her sentence because Sunshyne' s parents walked in and Sunshyne knew exactly what was coming out her mouth next. She was thankful they came in.

"Baby, we are about to get on out of here. You sure you won't need a ride back to the house?" Sunshyne had told her mom about her plans after the party, but Mrs. Morris just wanted to make sure before she left.

"No, Mother Dear. I will be fine. My ride should be here shortly. I'll hang out here for just a little bit longer."

"Alright, sweetie. Then we're gone. Good night, Chelle." Mr. Morris hugged both ladies, and Sunshyne's parents made their exit.

As soon as her parents walked out the door, her phone rang. The corners of her mouth immediately crept up. Michelle knew exactly who it was. "And he is right on cue. He must have seen your mom and dad walking to their car."

"Girl, whatever. He don't even know them. Let me go say goodbye to Ruben and Renae."

"I'll go grab Carlton so we can get on as well." They strode back into the main room. Sunshyne found the people she needed to speak to before she left. She walked out with Michelle and Carlton while Richard sat in the parking lot and watched her drive away with Kody.

Sunshyne

Sunshyne was pleased with the night Kody had planned them. They went to eat followed by the California Clipper, an intimate bar located near Chicago's Humboldt and Wicker Park neighborhoods. Kody noticed Sunshyne's face when they walked in. There weren't too many faces like theirs so he immediately told her, "Don't worry. You are going to enjoy yourself. Tonight's band is awesome."

The club hosted a jazz band playing modern and contemporary songs. They covered songs from lesser known artists as well as popular singers like Curtis Mayfield, Stylistics, and Dee Robinson. They also threw in a few of their own original pieces. Most of the crowd, including Kody and Sunshyne joined them at the stage when they played Alright by Ledisi.

She was shocked when he grabbed Sunshyne's hand to pull her to the dance floor. "I thought you didn't like dancing."

"I never said I didn't like to dance. I enjoy watching women dance the way you did to reggae music. Now come on and let me show you how to step. I hope you can keep up."

"I'm not the best but I am great at following as long as you know how to lead."

"Baby, I'm from Milwaukee. I better know how to step."

"You say that like you are from the Chi. Everyone knows the real steppers are from Chi Town."

" I'll show you better than I can tell you." Kody took her hand, and Sunshyne willing followed him to the dance floor.

Kody moved across the floor like he was gliding on air. He was a serious stepper. His eyes were closed while his feet moved effortlessly to the melodies of the band. The way he twirled and guided her was mesmerizing. He could have appeared on Stepping at Club 7 or Stepping into Heaven any Friday or Saturday night. Sunshyne followed every command he gave her with the flick of his wrist. There was one move when he spun her and brought her back into him. He held her close to him face-to-face, and she got stuck like a deer in headlights staring into his spellbinding eyes. They stayed on the dance floor as long as the band played their stepper's set. It seemed like they may have extended that portion of their show. There were a few more couples stepping, but none looked as good as Kody. Most of the patrons were *just* out there dancing. They probably didn't know anything about stepping but they were enjoying the music. After their assortment of stepper numbers, they went into a pop arrangement. Sunshyne and Kody took that opportunity to catch a breath and wet their whistle.

"You weren't playing when you said you knew how to step. I had to work hard to keep up with you. You definitely made me look good out there on the dance floor," she said wiping the sweat from her forehead with one of the cocktail napkins the waitress left with their drinks.

"Baby girl, I told you. I was introduced to this at a young age. Everyone in my family gets down on the dance floor. Well, everybody except Niko. He is the one that doesn't dance at all. I don't care what kind of music you play. You did a great job out there though. You talkin 'bout you can't step all that good."

"Well you are an excellent partner, and the band is nice. I would have never thought they would play any of those songs."

"Yea, one of my boys used to be part of a band that played here a lot. So I used to come listen to him play. Sometimes we would come down here after I closed up the shop some nights to catch some of the other talent that performed."

They talked and listened to music for a little while longer until Sunshyne couldn't hold her yawns anymore. They arrived at her place, and Kody walked her to the door. As they walked up to the building, she attempted to be inconspicuous looking around to see if she saw Richard anywhere around. She didn't see him anywhere, and this time she wasn't gonna miss the opportunity to get that kiss good night. Only this night it wasn't going to happen outside. It looked like he wasn't gonna miss out either. He leaned in to kiss her. She instinctively kissed him back.

As Sunshyne was about to invite him in, Kody spoke, "Good night pretty girl. I gotta be up in a couple hours to get my cousin to the airport so I better go."

She held back her slight hint of disappointment. "You stay on the move. When do you ever sleep?"

"My motto is, *You can rest when you die*. I want to take advantage of every minute I have while I'm here."

"I wish I had your energy. I had a wonderful time tonight. That place was amazing."

"Don't go telling everybody about it. I don't want to see all your Glenmont folks at our spot."

"Our spot, is it? Oh okay. No problem. I will keep *our* spot a secret. Now you go on, and I will see you tomorrow."

"Alright. Good night." He waited for her to get in and asked her to call and let him know she made it in her apartment safe and sound.

That night Sunshyne went to bed with a smile on her face. Before she closed her eyes she made sure she had a conversation with God. She had more in her than just a *Lord have mercy* or *Thank you Jesus* prayer tonight. This would not be quick or what some people call a microwave prayer.

Heavenly Father, I just want to say thank you. Thank you for being all that I need. Father, I have learned to trust you in all that I do. It isn't always easy. I remember all that I have endured, and you have been with me through it all. I can't thank you enough for bringing me to where I am today. I know I would have never made it here without you. I tried so many times to do things on my own without any guidance from you, and so many people have suffered unnecessarily because of my decisions. I vow that will never happen again as long as I can help it. You have given me the direction I needed when I was ready to run from my problems and when I wasn't sure what to do about the shop you told me to stick it out. Now we are flourishing. Father, now I come to you asking that you show me how to handle Richard and my sister's situation. I have allowed my emotions to control my actions in the past but I am asking you to help me do the right thing as far as they are both concerned. My first thought was to have my brothers holla at him but this morning Pastor Collins just preached about mercy. Still, I need to take care of things before he does something crazy. And I know my sister's business is hers, but that is my baby sister. Lord, please."

Sunshyne thought she needed more time with God, but He thought otherwise. Midway through her prayer, she heard Him speak to her, *"Be still, and let me handle it. I don't need your help with this one."* She was kinda shocked. She had gotten answers from God before but never this quick. He had never been so blunt with her before, or maybe she hadn't paid this much attention. Either way, she heard Him loud and clear. Now she knew that if He spoke, she'd better listen.

"Lord, I hear you and will follow your command by not handling anything on my own. I trust that you will protect me and Desiree. In your son's name. Amen." Sunshyne laid in the bed staring at the ceiling thinking about all that was going on around her until she finally dozed off to sleep.

Renae

Almost two weeks had passed since Ruben proposed to Renae. They set the date for next year. It was a tough decision for her. She contemplated getting married on her mom's birthday in May, or her grandmother's birthday whom she shared a birthday with in June. She decided not to be overshadowed by either of those somber dates. They would get married next July. She had discussed a destination wedding with Desiree but decided against that as well. She wanted to share her day with as many friends and loved ones as possible.

Ruben was all set to start school in August, and things were moving pretty fast with the purchase of the garage. She sat at the table eating her homemade BLT sandwich, drinking her freshly brewed iced tea with Muffin laid at her feet. Everything was going great. Had she still been living in the past she would have been waiting for the proverbial shoe to drop? Instead, she remembered the scripture her pastor often quoted. When she thought about what was happening in her life she believed the sun was rising and her morning had come. In the past, Renae defined love by what the men in her life gave her or did for her. The more she listened to Pastor Collins the more she realized that she wasn't going to find the love she expected in the men she sought after. They did things she once saw as love until she realized that they needed to show her they loved her no matter what day it was or the situation. This time she felt like God had finally allowed her to reap all the love she had sown throughout her life. The time she thought she had wasted giving her energy and love to no good men, was now returned to her. This was her time to get everything back from Ruben. It was not too late, and she wasn't going to be too scared to enjoy what He had planned for her.

Sunshyne

Sunshyne rolled over, and her clock read 9:30 a.m. She couldn't remember the last time she got to stay in bed this late but was glad she was able sleep in today. The children stayed with Marcus the night before so there were no mommy duties to fulfill this morning. She was glad her and Marcus had been getting along better and could actually parent without arguing all the time. She took care of some stuff for the shop before heading to the gym. She had taken more time off from working out than she realized, and she felt it. Everything seemed like a struggle for her. One of the many muscle-bound men seemed to have noticed it as well, or maybe this was his opportunity to flirt with her. Either way, he made his way over to the bench where she was doing her presses.

"Hey pretty lady. I was watching you and noticed you were having a hard time. I think you would be much better if you had a spotter. Maybe I could."

Before he could finish his sentence, Sunshyne heard a familiar voice that made her stomach crawl. "Naw, bruh. She's straight. I'll be the one to help her out if she needs some assistance."

Sunshyne sat up by this time to see Richard standing at the head of the bench. The handsome sculpted brotha looked at her ignoring the idiot that was speaking.

Sunshyne acted as if Richard was not standing close enough for her to inhale his Aqua Di Gio cologne. As the aroma filled her nostrils, she almost got swept back to a different time and place. That was not where she was today.

"I'm sorry. I didn't get your name."

"Kevin."

"Kevin, I think I might need a spotter. If you could just give me one second I would appreciate your help very much."

"No problem, sweetheart," he said placing emphasis on *sweetheart*.

When he walked away, Sunshyne quickly admonished Richard. "What the fuck don't you get about the whole leave me alone part? I am tired of the bullshit. I don't need you to help me workout. I don't need you to call me anymore. I don't need you sending me anything on social media. I'm gonna block you every time you create a new account. Listen very closely, I don't need you for anything else anymore. Stay away from me or."

"Or else what, Nette? What are you going to do? You gonna call your brothers on me, or maybe I need to be worried about your new boyfriend. I don't think you heard me clearly the last time I told you. I am not going to give up on us. We have been through too much."

"You are absolutely crazy for sure. I'm gonna tell you this though. Either you stay the hell away from me or you *will* regret it. That's all I got to say." She grabbed her water bottle and towel and headed towards the machine Kevin started using. She could feel Richard's eyes shooting daggers into her back, but she didn't turn around. She sat on the machine next to him and collected herself. She listened to what he thought they could do before it was time for him to leave.

Despite everything Sunshyne expressed to Richard about not wanting him anymore, he vowed he was not going to lose her. He would never lose her even though she moved on from having anything to do with him. Richard watched her work out until he couldn't take it any longer. He went to the locker room and let out his anger by punching the locker a few times and gathered his belongings and left.

Sunshyne wanted to get an order of protection against Richard. So after her workout, she immediately called an officer she knew at the Glenmont Police. She called Maurice to see what she needed to do. He was a detective on the force who had a crush on Sunshyne some time ago. They were cool so she knew he would give her the information she needed without being pressured into anything. He advised her to get an emergency order of protection. He also told her an emergency order of protection takes effect as soon as the judge approves it.

"No matter what you do, Sunshyne, please be careful and make sure you take care of this as soon as possible. You got this dude acting crazy. Whenever you're ready I can introduce you to one of our victim outreach officers."

"Thanks, Reese. I will make sure I get it done soon."

He made her promise before they disconnected the call.

On the way home from the gym she swung by her parents' house. She wanted to grab some of the leftovers from dinner yesterday. She heard her baby brother's deep voice as soon as she walked in the house. She just hoped he saved some of their mama's greens. She really wanted a piece of caramel cake but that would mess up everything she just burned at the gym.

"Hey Ma Dear. Hey y'all." Terrell and his boy Jamie were sitting at the table stuffing their faces with her mother's delicious cooking. "I didn't know you were here," she said speaking to Jamie. "I definitely heard your big mouth," she said to her brother as she slapped him on the back of his head. She made her way over to the sink where her mother was and kissed her on the cheek. “Where's daddy?”

“He's upstairs. He'll be down in a minute. Just moving a little slow this morning.” Her mother replied.

“Gotcha.” She turned to the men at the table as she opened the fridge. “I hope there's enough left for me.”

Terrell joked, “I think there's some tea left from yesterday.”

“Whatever.” She took the containers of food out the fridge. Her daddy stood in the kitchen doorway when she closed the refrigerator door.

“Hey Pops.”

“Hello, Mr. Morris.”

“Hey fellas.” “Hey baby. Fix daddy a plate while you're at it.” He said and kissed her on the forehead.

Sunshyne ate lunch and had some good laughs with her family. They talked about Ruben and Renae's engagement, how well the bar was going that Jamie and Terrell had started, and Terrell teased her about Kody. She pushed the events of the morning to the back of her head along with everything else surrounding Richard. She wanted to talk to her brother about it but she didn't want to talk about it in front of her parents.

Terrell looked at his watch. “Damn. Oops. I mean dang. It's almost two o'clock. We gotta get out of here.”

Sunshyne echoed his statement. “Me too. The kids will be home in a little while, and I need to get dinner started. Thanks for lunch.”

“Yes. Thanks for lunch Mr. and Mrs. Morris. Everything was delicious as usual.” Jamie grabbed his “to go” plate from the counter.

Sunshyne and Terrell hugged their parents and walked out to the driveway. Sunshyne stopped Terrell before he could get into his car. He saw the look on her face. "What's up, sis?"

"Before I tell you anything, I want you to promise you're not going to tell Mommy or Daddy."

"What, girl? You gonna give them another grandchild? Slow down and let me or Dee give them one." She gave him that look that he was playing too much, and she was trying to be serious. "Alright. No matter what it is you have my word. I won't say anything."

"You play too much, but y'all need to get working on it before you can't anymore." She stuck her tongue out at him like she would when they were younger. Any who. I called Reese to see how to get an order of protection on Richard. He won't leave me the hell alone. It seems like everywhere I turn he is there harassing me." Sunshyne went on to tell her brother about all the times she ran into him and how he was starting to scare her.

"Why the hell you wait so long to tell me? Don't worry about it. I'm gonna go holler at dude right now. I never liked the little squirrelly looking cat from jump. You go on and get your restraining order or whatever you want to call it but if I see him first, you won't be needing it."

"That is not why I'm telling you. Well, maybe one of the reasons," she said and winked. "I'm just sick and tired of his ass. I keep telling him but he don't get the picture."

"Well don't worry, sis. I got it under control. Trust me, you won't have to tell him again."

"Thanks, bro." They hugged and went on their way.

***

After Sunshyne put the kids to bed, she poured her a glass of wine and caught up on some of her shows she had on her DVR. She watched Scandal and was glad she didn't have the love complications Olivia continued to face anymore — in love with a married man that she couldn't ever seem to leave alone. She promised herself she would not stop anything new from blossoming because she couldn't move forward. Whether it was Kody or someone else, she knew she was ready.

Right on queue her phone lit up. It was a text from Kody. She had spoken to him on the way to the gym this morning but was happy to see his text.

Hey beautiful. Hope the rest of your day was great.

My day was eventful to say the least, but it was great. Got to spend a little time with my parents today so…

That's always a good thing. Leaving the shop on my way home. Didn't wanna call this late, but I just had to say good night.

Thanks sweetie. Good night yourself, sir. Sweet dreams.

Always of you. C ya in da morning.

Sunshyne closed her message app and sat for a few seconds grinning like a teenaged girl who was just asked to prom by her high school crush. As happy as she was about where they were headed she still had a nervous, uneasy feeling about what might happen with Richard. She couldn't stop thinking about him as much as she tried to push him out of her thoughts. She did not want to be the next headline. She had to take extra precautions from here on out.

Renae

Renae and Ruben were leaving from her dad's and Ms. Loretta's when his phone rang. It was Bruce's brother. He had some good news and some bad news. He had gotten a promotion and would be leaving the loan department within the next thirty days. He would still be able to push the loan through, but Ruben needed to move a little faster. Craig told him he would give him a couple days to think about it, and Ruben told him he would get back to him as soon as possible. He hung up the phone and explained to Renae what they spoke about.

"So what do you want to do?" She asked.

"Well, I you know I really want this but I also wanted to be a little more prepared at handling the business when I take it over."

"I'm sure Lester wouldn't mind helping out until you can get things figured out. Plus, I think you can take more technical classes to learn what you need instead of giving your money to any of these colleges or universities. I think I needed to get my degree in order to compete to get the job I have, but you on the other hand have no one to compete with. You are about to start your own business. Of course, you will need the basics, but we have enough people around us to help get you through it."

Ruben gave her a slight puzzled look, "Why did you wait until now to share all of that with me?"

"You were so excited with your plans and how you wanted to handle everything so I didn't want to bring you down. Now that everything is moving faster I want you to know that you should go ahead and get started. I don't think you need to wait. Talk to Lester and see what he thinks about staying around to show you everything he knows. If we need more, we can reach out to Michelle or Terrell. They both have successful businesses. Michelle agreed to help however she can and I'm sure Terrell wouldn't mind. We could ask Sunshyne as well. Like I said, we have enough people in our lives to get you through this. Don't let a piece of paper hold you back from what you really want."

"This is why I need you to be Mrs. Bradshaw. This evening I will go by the shop and sit down with Lester when I know he has slowed down. I will call the school and let them know I will not be enrolling. They can stop the process. Baby, I'm glad you think the way you do, but don't hold out on me next time. Even if it's not what I want because what I want ain't always gon be what's best for us. This ain't about me no more. It's all about us. You are my voice of reason when I'm not thinking straight. Don't let me step off the ledge."

"No problem, sir. Now let's get home. I am sure Muffin is crossing her legs at the door. We have been gone longer than I expected, and she hasn't been out since you left this afternoon."

***

Renae was in the kitchen cooking dinner when the doorbell rang. She looked through the peephole and saw both of Paul's sisters standing on her front porch. She knew this was not going to be good. Tanya visited her more than a few times which Desiree thought was weird, but Renae felt like her and Tanya were friends before she started dating Paul. They became closer once the relationship started. Kenyatta, on the other hand, never seemed to like Renae. She tolerated her because of her brother. It was never more than that in Renae's eyes. Once Paul passed, Kenyatta let her true colors show. She blamed Renae for everything that went wrong in the relationship despite the fact that she knew like the rest of Glenmont that Paul messed around with several women in and around the town. Eventually, he had a child with one of them. Honestly, she didn't care what Kenyatta thought about her. Now that she was standing on her porch with Tanya, Renae couldn't begin to imagine what the purpose of this visit was for.

She swung her front door open and Tanya burst out with an elated, "Hey girl, and before you start wondering what we're here for, Kenyatta wants to talk to you."

Renae stood right in the doorway without budging, looking directly at Kenyata and in an insistent tone, "What do you need to talk to me about? I have told the police and your entire family that I don't know anything about what happened to your brother."

"We know, Nae. That's why we're here. Can we come in off the porch? We," and she emphasized *we*, "want to talk to you but we don't want to have the conversation out here."

Renae reluctantly moved aside to allow the women to enter the house. Muffin started barking uncontrollably like she knew a demon just entered her house. Renae calmed her down and turned toward the women, "You can have a seat there." She directed them to the enclosed porch area. "Let me just turn down my food so it doesn't burn."

When she returned from the kitchen, Tanya didn't hesitate with why they were there. "So, Mama got a call from the police today. They told her they had arrested the person who killed Paul." Both Tanya and Kenyatta started to tear up. Renae went to the guest bathroom and returned with some tissue. She felt bad about what happened, but not enough to shed anymore tears over him.

"Did they tell her who it was? Do we know them?" Renae was extremely curious now. She knew it wasn't Ruben since they had been together most of the day, and he had left her a while ago. She started wondering if they had arrested Rufus. If it was him, she didn't think he would give them anything on Ruben. You never know what somebody might do in certain situations. Different scenarios were running through her head.

Her mind stopped wondering and she snapped back when she heard Tanya's voice become louder. "Did you hear what I said? They believe it was Kingston. I know you heard they raided his house a couple weeks ago. Well, they found the gun in the house. He told them he bought the gun from a crackhead. The only prints on the gun were his girl, Clarissa. They knew Paul had stuck him up weeks before his death. He had just gotten out from the raid. Yesterday they arrested him again. Looks like he ain't letting her go down for it."

Renae's mind was a little bit at ease, and she remembered hearing about him getting hit. Somehow he had purchased the wrong gun from somebody. "That's messed up. He got caught up like that. I'm sure your mother was happy to hear the news. Are they sure that's the right one?"

Kenyatta spoke. "They told Mama it was the one, and they also told her they should have no problem convicting him for it. Yes, she was happy. We all are. Anyway, I wanted to come by to apologize for the way I treated you after everything happened. I believed you and Ruben had something to do with it. Now I see you didn't."

Renae felt a tinge of deception. She would never tell them the truth about how their brother died. She really didn't know the entire truth herself. They would never know what she knew. She started to tell Kenyatta it was alright, but she let her finish saying what she came for.

"I also want you to know that I am sorry for the way I treated you when you and my brother were together. I knew the stuff he was doing to you was wrong, but still I always blamed you for the problems in the relationship. I never held him responsible for anything he did. Maybe that was because of what was going on in my life at the time. I allowed the same shit to happen in my life, whatever the case, I should have never treated you the way I did. I was one of the women they talk about when they say misery loves company. I'm not here to try to be your friend, I wanted to clear the air between us. I told Tanya I wanted to do it in a place where we could be face-to-face with no one else around. We probably should have called first; we figured you wouldn't have let us come by. Anyway, that was all I wanted. I'm gonna go."

Renae wasn't sure what to say to her. She wanted to acknowledge her apology for what it was; she knew that's as far as it was gonna go. Renae spoke what was on her mind because at this point she wanted them out of her house, "Kenyatta I hope this doesn't come off the wrong way. I appreciate everything you said, and we don't need any further problems. There is nothing else you and I need to say to each other. I'm glad y'all found out the truth about Paul. That's where it ends for me. I don't want to be rude but I need to get back to cooking my dinner." She waited for them to head towards the door. Kenyatta didn't hesitate. She went to the door and went straight to her car. Tanya and Renae said a few pleasantries before she left. She had hoped that she didn't say anything to ruin their friendship; she believed Tanya knew exactly how her sister had treated her all those years and how she felt about all of it.

She checked her food to make sure everything was alright and then she texted Ruben.

Won't tell you why but we got some celebrating to do tonight.

What's going on, baby?

I just said I'm not gonna tell you so don't ask again. Just hurry up and get here you will find out.

Alright then. I'll be there as soon as I can.

Renae poured a glass of wine and smiled. She hoped this didn't come back to haunt them.

Sunshyne

Sunshyne had a long week and was ready for the weekend. Not much was planned, and that was the best part about it. Usually she had a lot going on and it felt good to be able to do nothing—if that's what she wanted to do. Meechie was having a card party at her house tomorrow night, and she was more than welcome to stop through.

"You can also bring your Boo if you want."

"I'll see. I was planning on staying in the house and chillin' with the kids this weekend. They might make plans of their own and get ghost on me. I'll give you a call and let you know what I'm gonna do."

"Alright. That's cool." Meechie walked to the front and hollered back that she was gone. Sunshyne didn't hear her over the vacuum. She finished vacuuming and began cleaning her brushes and sterilizing her combs. She took the vacuum to the storage room, and when she came out Richard was standing in the middle of the room.

Sunshyne gasped with a quickness and her mind stuttered in confusion. She was stuck in time for a few seconds. Her brain signaled for her to move but her body was motionless. Once the two connected she yelled at him, "How the hell did you get in here?"

"The door, Nette. It was unlocked. Calm down. You don't need to be afraid of me."

"Why don't I? I would have never thought so before, but lately you have been acting crazy and making me feel extremely nervous around you. There is no reason why you should be here. In all actuality, there is really no reason why you should be at most of the places I have been seeing you, but yet and still, there you are. I told your ass to stay away from me, and I meant it. We don't have anything else to talk about. Just leave."

All of a sudden a seriousness came over his face that unnerved her. The smile fizzled out of his eyes, and the warmth that used to be there left. His eyes were narrowed and fixed. She measured the distance between where she was standing and her drawer. She knew she couldn't make it to grab the 380 in her drawer. She looked across the street and noticed the lights were still on at the shop. She thought it might be easier to get closer to the door that way she would draw some attention to herself. She took a couple steps to the door, "Bye Richard."

Richard grabbed her by the arm and slammed her into one of the salon chairs. Things were about to get ugly. During the time they were together he never put his hands on her. She realized he had lost it now. She prayed for something miraculous to happen—that somebody would walk towards the door. Normally, Kody would be there after the shop closed. He was at a track meet for one of the young men he mentored. She couldn't beat him in a fight, but she was not going down without a fight. She had to get close enough to her drawer to possibly reach her gun. She sat in the chair and her heart was racing. He started rambling, talking crazy, and pacing the floor.

"I'm sorry, baby, I didn't mean that. I don't want to hurt you. You know I love you. You know I wanted us to share our lives together, but you couldn't wait. You couldn't be patient and wait for me to get things together. I told you I was working on leaving Monica's ass. You had to ruin everything for us. Why couldn't you just hold on and let me handle everything? Look at how you got me acting. We are supposed to be together, living out my dreams. Instead you are making me hurt you when I don't want to."

She interrupted attempting to reason with him, "If you don't want to hurt me, let me go. We can walk away like none of this ever happened. It will be between me and you. I won't even."

He screamed and grabbed her. He pinned her shoulders to the chair, "That's the problem. I don't want us to go our separate ways. I want us to be together and you won't cooperate."

She started to say something else and he completely lost it. He clenched her throat and wouldn't let go. The deranged look in his eyes terrified her, and she could feel his hands getting tighter like a vice grip around her neck. Instinctively, she tried to fight back. She punched his chest and scratched his arms. She struggled to breath and her head began hurting. She could feel herself slipping into unconsciousness. This was not how she was going to die. She said a quick prayer and made one last effort to free herself from him. She dug her nails into his face and felt his flesh, and at the same time she kicked him as hard as she could in his groin. She thought it had been hard enough. He fell back into the case display of hair products and laid on the ground holding his crotch. Sunshyne tried to get out the door when he hit the floor, but he grabbed her leg and dragged her to the ground. She gathered her composure enough to grab one of their statuettes that had fallen from the counter and hit him over the head. He blacked out, but she hit him again to make sure. She made it to her drawer to get her gun, but it wasn't there. She remembered it was in her glove box. She had to get away from him before he came to and she could get the police there. She darted for the front door, and as she passed the front desk she noticed her keys on the counter. She grabbed them, ran out the door and locked it behind her. She ran across the street to the shop. Niko was in there with one of the barbers and a couple clients.

As soon as she entered the shop the fellas stopped talking and looked her way. Niko could tell something was wrong as soon as he turned towards her. He jumped up. "What's going on, Sweetheart?"

She could barely talk, "Call the police please."

"What is going on?" He became more insistent this time.

"Please just call them. Somebody came into the shop and attacked me."

"What the hell? Where are they at?" He got ready to run out the shop but she stopped him before he could get to the door. He looked closer at her and saw the bruising already forming on her neck. He let it go for now.

She begged him again to call the police, and he finally gave in and followed her directions. After he called the police, he immediately called his brother. He didn't answer so he texted him and told him to call him as soon as possible.

Niko calmed down and inquired what happened. Sunshyne finally started telling him the story when she heard the sirens and saw the cars pulling up in front. The men followed her across the street to meet the police. Richard was still on the floor knocked out cold when she unlocked the door for the police. One of the officers called for an ambulance while the other questioned Sunshyne to determine what had happened. She heard him ask for two ambulances. She told him she was okay, and there was no need to call one for her. Everyone tried to convince her to go but she refused. Niko stood right there next to her while she answered their questions. He stepped away for a brief period to talk to his brother. When he came back the officer finished his questions and Sunshyne tried to reach Terrell. He didn't answer so she called Damon.

Lauren answered, "Hey sis. What's going on with you?"

"Hey girl. Where's Damon?"

"He's coming. Is everything alright? Hold on. Here he is."

Damon got on the phone, "Hey sis. What's happenin?"

"Don't get all excited. I am fine. Richard came in the shop on me tonight. To make a long story short his ass is laid out cold on my floor."

"What the fuck? What happened?"

"Can you meet me at the station? I can tell you everything there. They want me to come down so they can take my report."

"Okay. I'll meet you there. Have you called Mom and Dad?"

She almost took his head off, "No and don't call them just yet. I don't want them worrying for nothing. We can stop by there once we leave the station."

He was reluctant but he agreed. "I'll be there as soon as I can." He hung up the phone, told Lauren the little bit he knew and started getting his stuff. She told him she was coming with. They both left and headed to the Glenmont Police Station to figure out what had happened at the shop tonight.

Lauren and Damon were at the station when Sunshyne walked in with an unknown man. Sunshyne saw the look on their faces as soon as she entered the building. She introduced everyone, "Niko, this is my brother and his wife, Lauren. This is Niko. He and his brother just opened the shop across the street from us. The one I gave you the flyer for."

The fellas shook hands. Then Damon told him, "Yea. That must have been your brother I met. I couldn't make the grand opening. My son and I stopped in last week."

"Okay. Cool. I hope you'll be back."

"For sure." The officer that was at the shop walked up with a plain clothes detective. The detective's face was familiar to Sunshyne and Damon. They grew up with him and he always had a crush on Sunshyne. They ended up dating when they got older but nothing serious came of it. They both realized they were on different tracks, and she was stuck on Marcus.

"Hey, Nette. Damon." Maurice Taylor had been the detective assigned to her case. He directed his attention to Sunshyne. "Are you ok? The officer said you refused to go to the hospital."

"Yea, Reese. I want to take care of this, and then I'll go. I need some water if you got some." He instructed the officer to grab a few bottles of water. "Nette, let's go upstairs so we can talk, and I'll take your full report."

"Alright, but I want Damon to come with me."

"Of course. That's no problem." He pointed to the stairs so they could go up to his office. Just as they started to leave, Niko came rushing in the door.

"Hey, sweetheart. Hey everybody." He turned his attention back to Sunshyne. "Are you alright? What happened exactly?"

"I'm fine. I'll tell you everything later. Let me get this over with so we can get out of here."

"Okay. I will be right here when you come back."

Terrell returned her call. She didn't want to answer. She asked Lauren to call him and Desiree for her. She wanted them to meet them at their parents' house in about an hour or so. Sunshyne and Damon went upstairs with Maurice. About forty-five minutes later they walked back down the stairs.

"Like I said, Nette, you have my number. Call me with anything else you can think of. He will go to court in the morning and likely get a bond. Since you didn't get the chance to get your order, the judge will definitely enter one for you tomorrow. If he comes around again or even if he calls, make sure you call us immediately."

"Thanks, Reese. I will be there in the morning; see you then." She turned to Damon, "I'm sure you and Lauren need to get home. I appreciate the both of you coming down."

"We're cool. We are going to swing by the house to check on the kids and meet you at Mamas." He looked at Niko, "Can you make sure she gets there?"

"No problem, bro. I definitely will."

Sunshyne thanked Niko for all he had done that evening. He said he was going to go back to the shop and make sure everything was good. He asked if she wanted him to check on hers as well while he was there. She gave him the keys and asked him to pull the gate in front of the door. She could get the keys back from him tomorrow. When they got in the car she stared straight. "If you don't mind I'd like to chill until we get to the house. I don't want to keep telling this story over and over again."

"Sure, baby. No problem."

Sunshyne called MJ and told him to make sure he and his sisters ate. She told him she would be late getting home. She laid her head back and felt Richard's hands closing around her neck again. She couldn't believe it had come to this. She was glad she got away from him when she did. Tears began streaming down her face like a slow running faucet.

Kody looked over at her but didn't say a word. He held her hand giving it a comforting squeeze.

***

Everyone was at the house by the time Sunshyne arrived. Michelle's car was even out front. There was no reason to tell Lauren to call because she was sure Desiree called her. She walked in the house and was comforted by her mom and reprimanded by her dad.

Her mother grabbed her and held her tight. "Baby, are you ok? What happened?"

"Yes. What the hell happened, and why didn't you tell us what was going on the other day when you were here? This shit right here is crazy." Mrs. Morris tried to calm her husband down.

"Baby, don't get so worked up. Come on have a seat and let her tell us what happened."

He father sat down in his chair. Sunshyne shot her baby brother an evil look. She knew he was the one who said something about the other day. He just shrugged his shoulders as to say he was sorry. She rolled her eyes at him and made a note to deal with him later. She formally introduced Kody to her parents. She told her parents everything that had transpired with Richard. How he popped up in the same places she would never expect. She recalled the episode that took place at the gym the other morning. The more she talked she began to choke up. She could barely get her words out without tearing up. She paused for a minute and got herself together. She fought through the tears to finish telling everybody what she had to endure earlier that night. She could see everyone in the room becoming more angered. Terrell and Damon were over in the corner having their own conversation. Sunshyne could just imagine what they were talking about.

Everybody else had a bunch of questions for her. Kody pretty much sat to the side texting on his phone. He didn't want to get in the way while she was with her family. He would wait and talk to her more when they were alone.

After a few minutes, Mr. Morris shut it all down. "Nette needs to get to the hospital so they can finally check her out."

She knew he wasn't going to be happy with her response, but she said it anyway. "Daddy, I'm just going to go home and get some rest. I don't feel like being bothered with a bunch of people right now. If I need to, I will go in the morning, but for now I'm going home. I need to call Meechie to tell her what happened and see if she can cover my book for me tomorrow."

Her mother saw the look on his face and knew he was about to say the wrong things so she jumped in before he could say anything. "Go on and get your rest. We will see you in the morning. What time did they say court started?"

"9:30, but you don't have..."

She couldn't get another word out before he mother cut her off. "That's what you not gonna do. You're not going to tell me what me and your daddy can and can't do. Now, we're gonna let you go on home and not go to the hospital, but we will see you in the morning at the courthouse. If you need a ride you can let us know."

"Okay, Ma Dear. I probably will because I'm not going back to the shop tonight. I really just want to go home, take a hot bath and go to bed."

Everyone gave their hugs and said their goodbyes. They told Sunshyne to get some rest. Damon told her he would call and check on her after court because he couldn't take any time off. She told him not to worry about it. She appreciated him coming out with her tonight. Once their front yard was empty, Mr. and Mrs. Morris cut off the porch light and went to bed. Mr. Morris fussed a little more with his wife about the situation before they went to bed. She was used to it so she let him express his feelings and knew he would eventually lay down.

Sunshyne

Sunshyne and Kody were both quiet for the short ride to the shop to get her purse. He wanted to feel her out and see what was going on in her head. He didn't want to be too harsh. He wanted her to know she could talk to him about anything. He was not there to judge her. He was working on becoming the one she shared everything with, and he wanted her to start now.

"Sweetheart, I know we haven't been seeing each other for a long time, but I want you to know that I'm here. I know it sounds cliché, but I mean it when I say you can talk to me about anything. I want you to feel safe with me no matter what is going on with you. Had I known all of that was going on with that dude I would have handled things a little differently. I felt some tension with you a couple of times after we ran into him, but I chalked it up to him being your ex."

"I didn't want to get you involved in my nonsense. I have always tried to handle things on my own and work them out myself until I know I can't. I still have a hard time relying on others even though it has hindered more than helped me in the past. I really am working on it though."

"Well, Sweetie, I'm trying to be here to handle things with you. Even though the circumstances that brought me to Glenmont were not the best, the short amount of time I've been here has been great. Most of that is because of you. As long as you're straight with me, we are going to be in this together. I'm not gonna let anything happen to you."

Sunshyne hesitated. She wanted to share more than she had now that all this was out in the air. They were about to pull up to her place. She wanted to go on and have the conversation tonight. "Let me go upstairs and check on the kids. We can go somewhere quiet and talk, or we can sit here"

"That sounds cool. We can stay here so you're not far from the kids."

Sunshyne went upstairs to make sure her children had done what she instructed. Maia was in her room reading, and the older two were in the living room on their phones. She was glad she had taken a scarf from her mom's. She didn't need them to see the bruising on her neck that would spark too many questions. She grabbed her and Kody a bottle of water out the fridge and told the kids she would be downstairs talking to a friend of hers but would be back up before they were in bed.

Kody was on the phone when she got back to the car. Marcus had texted and called her earlier so she took the time to text him back. She told Marcus she was alright and would call him in the morning. She called Meechie also to tell her what happened at the shop. She gave her the full story and said she had to be at court in the morning. Meechie asked had she been to the hospital yet. She told her was okay and may go in the morning. She told her nothing was really damaged but asked if she could get there early to make sure everything was straightened. Meechie would have Lollie meet her to get everything in order. She also told her she would handle her clients and to take it easy. They both agreed she wouldn't be at the card party, and Meechie would stop by to check on when she could. Kody was done with his call by the time she got off the phone.

She sat there quiet for a minute then sighed and took a deep breath like she was sitting in the principal's office and was about to confess to smoking weed in the girl's bathroom.

"I don't know where to start so I'll just start here. You can ask whatever questions you need."

He smiled at her, "I'm all ears."

She continued staring out the front of the car. She started out telling him about her and Marcus. How they were basically never a couple and just the parents of their three children. He wanted her to look at him when she talked so he took his two fingers and gently turned her face towards him. It wasn't just so that he could look into her eyes but he wanted her to see the sincerity in his. She admitted that neither one of them were the best parents they could be but after the chain of events that happened last year they both woke up and started getting their stuff together. She gave him a brief summary of what happened and went on to tell him about her relationship with Richard. She knew it wasn't right, and she didn't have an excuse for why she got involved with him or even stayed with for that matter. She allowed her feelings to get caught up in the wrong person. She shared Maia's accident with him. As she reflected back at the thought, she began to tear up again but told him today her tears were filled with joy. She silently thanked God for bringing her family through that moment. She finally got to the part when she lost their baby and realized that he was never gonna leave this wife. That was the point when she accepted the fact that everything he was promising her about their future was all lies. Despite the numerous times her pastor preached about it, she could not see him for the person he was, even though he showed her time and time again.

"So here we are in the present." She had turned to face front, and he again brought her face back towards him. She looked him in his eyes, "He couldn't accept the fact that I wasn't going for his bullshit anymore and started popping up on me trying to win me back. You know about the one time he popped up at the restaurant we were in but there were several other times he just happened to be at the same place I was. It seemed odd to me and he acted unstable to me. I mentioned it to Michelle; she laughed it off as if I was being paranoid. Then the other day he finally went too far while I was at the gym working out. I had talked to the officer you met at the station about getting an order of protection, but I wasn't able to get the process started before tonight. I told my brother, in part, so he knew what was going on and also so that he would do something, if given the chance. In a way, I'm glad it happened like this, otherwise, my baby brother would be the one sitting in jail."

"Again, I wish I would have known all of this was going on with you, but I get it. From this day forward, Ms. Nette Morris, please don't keep anything like this from me again. I realize that not enough time has passed for you to completely trust me, but I am willing to take baby steps. Just know that I am not gonna hold anything back that you want to know or that I think is going to seriously affect our relationship. I hope you will do the same. I plan on sticking around for a while, baby girl, and I promise you I don't have a wife and children tucked away anywhere. Baby, you had me at *Hello, my name is Sunshyne Jeanette*, and I want to know everything there is to know.'"

Her eyes lit up thinking back to that day, and a warm smile covered her face remembering how she fumbled with her name the evening she met him. "I smile whenever I think about you, and I'm extremely happy when we spend time together. Going through this may get rough because I'm sure he is not going down without a fight. He didn't walk away easily. I am sure he will make this hard for me too."

"Well if you let me, I will go through this with you. I think I can handle myself."

A faint smile burst through her lips, "I will. Tomorrow, let me handle this one with my family. My sister and Michelle, if not my brother too, will want to get together to talk about this afterwards.'

"That's no problem. I will make sure to check on you after. Now I think you should go up and get your rest. What time do you have to be out there tomorrow?"

"He is supposed to be out there by 9:30 a.m. I'm gonna make sure I am out there early so I don't miss anything."

He grabbed the handle to open the door, "Come on, Sweetheart. 'I'll walk you to the door."

Sunshyne followed suit. She swung her door open and exited the car very cautiously. Her body was hurting and she was exhausted. She was glad that she knew for sure that Richard was nowhere near her house. When they got to the door he grabbed her by the waist and pulled her close to him. She could instantly feel he wanted her as much as she wanted him. He pressed his lips against hers. It was soft and comforting in a way she could never express verbally. He held her tight and continued to console her body the best way he could, for right now, and she welcomed every bit of it. Although it lasted only seconds, her back relaxed and her shoulders didn't seem as heavy as they were minutes before.

They said their good nights, and Sunshyne went upstairs to the kids. MJ and Mariah were still on the couch when she opened the door. With the day she had, she was glad to be back at home with them. She checked on Maia who was knocked out. She turned off her lights and went back to the front with her older two. *Which Way is Up* was playing On Demand. This was one of the few old movies they would watch with her no matter how many times they saw it.

Mariah looked at her funny, "Mom, are you gonna take off your scarf?"

"Uh... uh. I'll take it off when I go to the room and get ready for bed. I just want to watch the movie before you fall asleep which probably won't be much longer."

"Why you so worried about her scarf? You act like you're her mama. Granny is probably at home with Granddad. Let's just watch the movie."

Mariah gave her older brother a shove, "and I don't think you miraculously turned into Daddy."

"Both of you hush and watch the movie!"

The kids quieted down just in time for Leroy's dad to come out the house fussing about the chicken in the refrigerator. She laid back on the couch, and Mariah laid with her feet on MJ's lap, and her head in Sunshyne's. "This is what it's all about," she thought to herself.

Sunshyne

Court had gone as most expected it to go. They went through the preliminaries. The judge expressed his outrage to Richard and his attorney and was going to hold him with no bond, but his attorney argued that he had no criminal record and had lived in the community all his life. Richard was given a high bond and taken back to lock up. The judge warned that if he violated the order, he would keep him with no bond. After court she got together with Michelle and Desiree. Of course, they had a thousand and one questions, opinions, and plans for Richard. She didn't get too bothered by what they had to say because she knew it was all in love. Michelle told Sunshyne that the next time she told her about a crazy man stalking her, she wouldn't brush it off. They stayed for a few hours while the kids were out with Marcus shopping. After Michelle and Desiree left, she spoke with Kody for a while. She decided to cook dinner so the kids could hang out with her when they got home. She didn't do much. She made chicken, beef, and shrimp for tacos or nachos, whichever the kids decided they wanted. She set up a taco bar on the counter. She blended some virgin margaritas for the kids but she would probably have a couple of real ones. She texted Marcus not to feed them because she had cooked.

Marcus came up this time when he dropped them off instead of waiting outside for them to get in the house. Maia came running up the stairs first. She was always excited when she went shopping with her dad because he got her whatever she asked for. Sunshyne believed the little girl knew she had him wrapped around her finger.

"Look what Daddy bought me," she pulled item after item out of her Justice bag. "Look, he bought me a *Black Girls Rock* t-shirt."

Next she went to a Finish Line bag and pulled out two boxes of gym shoes. By now everyone else had made it up the stairs. "Oh. These are for you, Mommy. I told Daddy you needed a new pair of shoes to match mine so he bought them for you. He said you would pay him back when we got home."

Sunshyne looked at Marcus with a raised eyebrow. He laughed and looked at Maia, "I was just joking, baby. Your Mommy doesn't have to pay me back. She just has to make sure that y'all dress like twins when she wears them."

"Ooh yes, daddy. That's a good idea." The older two just laughed.

MJ interrupted and asked what she had cooked. She ran down the list.

"Good because Daddy said we had spent too much money at the mall, and we had to wait until we got back home to eat."

Sunshyne and Marcus looked at each other and just smiled. "You are welcome to stay and eat. I thought we would just hang out and watch movies. It's MJ's turn to choose."

"Yea, Daddy stay. Mommy's food is good, and you haven't eaten all day either."

"Alright, baby. I can stay for a little while."

Sunshyne sent the kids to take their stuff to their rooms and wash their hands. She and Marcus got a chance to have a brief conversation about what happened.

"I'm glad you are ok. Just give me the word, and I will make sure ol' boy is handled."

"I'm gonna tell you like I told my brothers, leave him alone and let the people handle it."

"Yea, ok. Whatever you say." He rolled his eyes and went to the kitchen to wash his hands and get his food.

The kids were ready to eat. She ushered them into the kitchen so they could fix their plates. They ate, laughed, and had a good time. MJ chose *All about the Benjamins* and *Fast and Furious II*. Kody and Sunshyne texted a few times until she told him that she would call him before she went to bed. Marcus said he had to leave halfway through *All about the Benjamins*. Sunshyne couldn't remember the last time they had hung out like that but she was glad he stayed as long as he did. It helped to keep her mind off of what she was going through, if only momentarily. Mariah and Maia went to their rooms after their dad left. They never liked to watch any of the *Fast* movies when he chose them. Sunshyne didn't either but she stayed in the living room with her first born. She wasn't really into the movie and eventually went to her room as well.

She was going to text Kody. Instead she laid there enjoying the peace and quiet until she succumbed to sleep.

Renae

Renae was up early Sunday morning so she decided to cook her man a hearty breakfast before church. He went into the club last night so she went ahead and let him sleep until breakfast was ready, or so she thought. She was standing at the stove when he snuck up behind her and wrapped his arms around her waist.

He kissed her on the neck, "Good morning, Baby."

She jumped a little from being startled. She turned around and slapped his chest with the towel she was holding, "Mr. Bradshaw, what is wrong with you? I've told you about doing that."

"I'm sorry, Sweetheart." He spun her around and planted a kiss on her lips while he cupped her butt.

"Don't start. We gotta eat so we can get ready for church. I want to be on time so I don't miss the choir."

"Alright. Alright. I'll wait until after church. For now I'll take my eggs scrambled light with American cheese."

"Ha. Will you now? Well, back up then so I can fix them just the way you like them."

Ruben sat at the table and waited patiently for his food. He wanted to take her to the bedroom. He opted to leave her alone in order to get to church.

***

Renae made it to church well before it started. She and Ruben could've had a little fun before they left this morning, but she pushed the thought out of her head. She thought maybe it was a holiday since church was so empty. It seemed like there were more members sitting in the choir stand than there were in the congregation. She didn't see Sunshyne or Michelle in church yet. Sunshyne normally got to church late, but Michelle and Carlton were always on time. Before she made it to her seat Maia and Bryson both came running to the back of the church. The rest of the crew was close behind. Sunshyne stopped to talk to Sister Johnson on her way to her seat. She tried to finish the conversation before Deacon Marshall came up. Sister Johnson kept going on about her niece who is finishing law school that she didn't have time to leave. Deacon Marshall had the creepiest hugs and most of the young women tried to stay away from him during fellowship.

The church filled. Renae realized she doesn't get to church early at all. She made a mental note that she needed to work harder on that. After a few minutes passed, the musicians started playing for the entry of New Living's choir. After the choir sang and the deacons finished devotion the choir started out with the song *Your Will* by Darius Brooks. One of the nurses came and stood right by Renae. She knew, matter of fact, the whole church knew this was about to send her over the top, and she didn't disappoint them. This was one of her favorite songs, and now she was definitely glad she got there early enough.

The choir usually sang two songs before Pastor Collins came to the podium to preach but that wasn't going to be the case today. By the time he got the church calm, he almost didn't have enough time to get his sermon in. There were plenty of times that the church simply had a worship service but it looked like there was a word for the church today.

"I didn't think y'all were gonna let me get up here to give you this word I have for you. I guess I say, if you let me have just fifteen minutes of your

time' so much you finally took me up on it." He turned toward the choir, "Thank you, choir, for ushering the spirit into this place. Thank you, deacons. Thank you, worship team for setting us up with an atmosphere of worship. Now if you would open to Isaiah 41, starting at verse ten it reads, 'So don't worry, because I am with you. Don't be afraid, because I am your God. I will make you strong and will help you; I will support you with my right hand that saves you. All those people who are angry with you will be ashamed and disgraced. Those who are against you will disappear and be lost. You will look for your enemies, but you will not find them. Those who fought against you will vanish completely. I am the Lord your God, who holds your right hand and I tell you, 'Don't be afraid. I will help you.' Let's read that again. 'Don't be afraid. I will help you.''' Today I want to talk to you on the subject of 'He will be with us through it all.'" He prayed and began his sermon.

"Sometimes you're going on about your way through life and things get dark. When we go through those dark times you have to go to his Word and remember His promises to get us through those dark times. We all have issues we go through. He never promised you wouldn't go through anything, but He did promise that He would be there with us always. Sometimes our connection with Him is not what it should be, and we don't realize how He is working on our behalf. I should have gotten a few more amens right there but I will take what I can now. It is the strength of God that gets us through our challenges. There will be challenges that try to set us back, but if you trust God to help, you will make it to the other side. Every morning you wake up you are facing something new because you are moving into another position, a new area in your life. You will continuously

face new things but if you go back to verse 10 you will know that God is telling you not to be scared. Depend on him because he will help you get through. Most of the time when we deal with our issues we are told to be still and allow God to take care of it for us. As the songstress Yolanda Adams tells us, 'The battle is not yours. It is the Lord's.'"

A few of the choir members shouted *hallelujah* and *preach pastor. "I knew I wouldn't get a lot of help right there because too many times we try to do it on our own. We don't trust the Lord. There are days when we wonder why we even had to deal with that particular situation, or why God rewards us instantly at other times. Remember the man with leprosy. He went to Jesus begging for healing. Jesus spoke to him and then reached out his hand to touch him. The leprosy left immediately. Then there was a woman in Mark chapter five with an issue of blood. All she wanted to do was to get to Jesus. Once she got to Him she was immediately healed."*

He paused from the sermon for a moment to instruct the congregation to turn to their neighbor to tell them immediately, *"If you keep your focus on Jesus your blessings will be instantaneous. Still there are times when He has to get us ready for what He has for us. He wants you to stop focusing on everything and everybody other than Him. He has to remind us that He will bring us out of our situation if we just believe in Him. In Acts 2 He used Luke to remind the people of Israel that He blessed them through the miracles Jesus performed before."* He pointed out how they had previously seen them for themselves, and if He did it then He would do it now.

He continued on with his sermon. Several members agreed with the points he made. Renae sat back and evaluated her life. She knew he had continuously blessed her life. She just looked at today's word as another confirmation that He would continue to grant her heart's desires as long as they were in agreement with His will. She knew she couldn't leave that part off anymore.

Pastor Collins brought her back to the sermon when he went into his final point. *"We have to go through some situations in order to remember that it is God who takes care of you. Deuteronomy tells us how the trip from Egypt to the Promise Land should have taken the children of Israel three to six months. Instead, it took them forty years simply because they didn't believe God's word when He told them He would never leave them. Some of us, like them, have been on a journey much longer than we have needed to be. There is some stuff that we don't ever plan to go through again. The tears you shed for that last situation will not happen again, but you find yourself repeatedly losing sleep over the same things asking yourself when will your morning come. On occasions God has to take you through some of those things to remind you that He is the one who takes care of you. He brought you through the lonely nights. He brought you through heartache and pain. Still, we wonder why God had to take us through painful experiences. You have to believe that He has no interest in making our lives bad. Once you learn to put down your pride and give God the glory for what you've achieved He will bless you. You won't have to repeat the same hardships once you are honest and admit that you don't deserve the credit for where you are. Never forget that wherever he takes you, He will be with you through it all. He promised never to leave us or forsake us."*

The congregation got on their feet clapping and shouting. Sunshyne just sat in her seat thinking back over all that she had been through and knew had it not been for Him on her side she would not be sitting here today. She silently praised Him giving thanks for where she was right now. She wanted to believe that she was ready for what He had in store for her next. All she knew was that no matter what it was she was going to make herself available. She wanted everything He had for her from this day forward.

By now Pastor Collins opened the doors of the church and directed the deacons to place the chairs at the front of the church. No one was moved to join so he prayed for the congregation and advised church was dismissed after the offering. Sunshyne met up with Michelle and Renae outside of the church.

"Nette, Dee told me about what happened the other day. I'm glad you're okay. They should have kept his crazy ass in jail. You know I'm gonna make sure I look at everything that comes through the office on this one." She gave Sunshyne a hug.

"Thanks girl. I wish they had kept him too. Hopefully he won't try nothing else now that he knows me, and the court ain't playing with him."

"Nette, I gotta run, but what are you doing later?" Michelle asked.

"You know I definitely gotta go by moms for dinner today. She would have a fit if I did anything else. I think when we leave there I may be going to the movies with Kody."

"Alright. Call me if you don't. The kids and I will come over for a little while."

"I will."

The three ladies went their separate ways. Sunshyne got in the car and drove to her parents' house listening to the kids argue as usual, rubbing her neck thinking about the other day and remembering how both her and Maia were living and breathing after their tragic experiences. She knew she would never be able to thank Him enough, but she was glad He had been with her and her family though it all.

Seven months later…

Renae was getting ready for Desiree's birthday dinner. Ruben was helping his dad finish putting down new carpet in their guest room and would meet her at the Morris' when he was done. She took this opportunity to confirm what she already knew. She had not had the chance to make it to the doctor's office so she bought one of the over-the-counter tests. She was excited, and at the same time she was a little nervous. Ruben had finally got everything in order to take over the garage so she didn't want to add to his plate. She knew that she was going to have to tell him and that both of them shared the responsibility, but she just hoped he would be as happy as she was.

When she exited the bathroom, she knew for certain her and Ruben were going to be parents. She stood in front of the mirror on her dresser holding her stomach. She promised herself she would call Monday to make an appointment with her doctor. After the brief moment of celebration, Renae remembered the miscarriages she had while she and Paul were together. She prayed that it had no bearing on her body and that it wouldn't keep her from having children with the man she was going to spend the rest of her life with.

"Oh my God," she thought to herself. She could not walk down the aisle with any type of belly in her wedding gown. She was going to have to move the wedding up. She couldn't think about all that right now. For now, she was headed to celebrate the life of her friend. She would figure out what was going on with the life growing inside of her after she talked to her doctor and Ruben.

If you have enjoyed *When Will My Morning Come* and *Through It All*, be on the lookout for *You Can't Hide*, the final installment of Sunshyne and her girls. Here is just a little of what you can look forward to.

YOU CAN'T HIDE

Teddy Pendergass said it best in his famous 1977 hit, *You Can't Hide From Yourself*. Wherever we go in life, we cannot run from who we are. We take everything about who we are with us on our journey through life. Our past has great influence on our present and future if not dealt with properly. We can try to suppress certain events, dismiss our actions, or leave individuals in our past, but if we don't deal with them they will come back around in our lives. It may not happen how you expect it, but you can trust it will return one way or another – good or bad.

In *You Can't Hide,* the characters find out that what is meant for you will eventually materialize if you trust and listen to your heart or how the circumstances of your past resurface if they are not dealt with. Regardless of what it is, you will see that they are not able to hide from it. This book will take you on highs and lows, and you will share laughs, joy and tears with the characters.

Desiree

Desiree could not believe she had fought traffic for over an hour to come downtown to the office only for the client to cancel their meeting ten minutes before it was to start. Lake Shore Drive was bumper to bumper and at a crawl the entire ride down. She would have ridden Metra if it wasn't Friday. She wanted to be able to leave work when she was ready. She didn't want to have to wait for the train. They didn't run as frequent during the day so fighting through rush hour traffic was the only option. She would have gotten a ride with Jerome, but he was up and out early this morning. She understood the cancellation by her client. He couldn't help it that his first born was ready to enter the world today, but it still didn't make her feel any better. Since she was in the office, she figured she would go ahead and make good use of her time. She needed to prep for a few depositions and review a few briefs her paralegal sent her the other day. She really didn't like working a full day on a Friday and believed you work hard during the beginning of the week so you can coast into the weekend. She was here, and there was no need to waste that drive. She finalized a couple of the briefs and responded to a few emails before running over to Panera to grab some turkey chili and Fugi apple salad with chicken. She wanted an agave lemonade, but it seemed like they were always out of it. When she got back to her office, the mail clerk had already delivered the mail and placed it on her chair. She tossed the stack of envelopes on her credenza and would look at it later.

About an hour into working on the Thillerman deposition, she got a text from Jerome. He was thinking about her and suggested they grab a bite to eat when she was done. She texted him back and told him she had just eaten but would be done in a couple hours and they could go from there. She wanted to finish prepping for the deposition, but half way through her mind became overloaded.

She called Jerome back, "Hey, My Love. I am ready to get out of here. I think I've done enough work for the day."

"Alright, Baby. I am headed back that way from a meeting with one of the suppliers. Are you ready to eat now?"

"No. How about we just go somewhere for a drink or two. I need something to help me relax." She sounded like she was expending energy with every word spoken.

"I can think of something better than some Hennessy to help you relax, and you may still be feeling a little drunk in love afterwards." Jerome always tried to be flirtatious, but after it came out he felt like it sounded corny. So did Desiree, but she always gave him a little chuckle though.

"Do you ever get enough?"

He interrupted her before she could say another word, "I can never get enough of your sweet pussy. If it wasn't so good, I wouldn't want it all the time."

"Well then maybe if you behave yourself you can get a treat when we get home."

Get home. The words rolled off her tongue so easy. She struggled with it for some time. Jerome wouldn't give up. She spent most of her time with him and couldn't understand why she wanted to continue to pay rent when she didn't have to. More importantly, he wanted her with him all the time. She wanted it too. She finally decided to move in with him and rent out her condo. She was a little apprehensive at first because she still held onto some of the scars and bad memories she had from living with Billie. However, it was much easier for her to give in once she convinced herself he was the one who had the flowers delivered to her condo. She knew she needed to move on and let them go. She was just thankful that Jerome was very patient with her. She shared a little about her relationship but never gave him the full story.

"Then I am going to be the teacher's pet. Maybe you'll teach me a few things while you're at it too. I'll be at your office in about ten minutes. Getting off the highway at Washington. I'll see you in a minute."

"Ok, Sweetie. I'm gonna start shutting down, and I'll be waiting for you."

They hung up the phone, and Desiree started getting her stuff together. She put the Thillerman file in her bag so she could work on it over the weekend. On her way out of the office she noticed the mail she threw on the credenza. She grabbed it and shoved it in her bag as well. Little did she know, the contents of one of the envelopes was about to turn her world upside down and take her back to a chapter in her life she thought she had closed.

Sunshyne

Sunshyne and Kody were going strong. They'd been dating for almost a year and she welcomed every minute of it. He fit right into the family like he had been a part of it forever. Her dad and brothers accepted him much easier than they had anyone else she had brought around. He had been by her side through the long, exhausting trial. Richard had refused to take the agreement his attorney and the state's attorney had worked out and took it to trial. Sunshyne couldn't understand why he would gamble like that. Everybody in town knew he was going to jail. It was just a matter of how long. It seemed the judge was upset Richard had put everyone through an unnecessary trial that he gave him the maximum sentence of fifteen years. She told him she wished she could have given him longer because he had attempted to take Sunshyne's life and leave three children motherless. She was happy that was over and she was able to move on with her life.

They had an extended weekend getaway planned. It would just be the two of them away from any and everything. The kids were going to be with her parents tonight, and Marcus would pick them up for the weekend. She told the older children not to call her unless it was an absolute emergency. She told her baby girl her phone would not be working where she was going and if she needed anything to call her dad. She had a feeling that wasn't going to go over too well but tried it anyway. Sunshyne not only felt bad about leaving the kids, she felt even worse for wanting to get the break. Even though they had not been away from each other unless they spent the night with family or friends, this was still wrong in her head. Everyone told her to go on and have fun, and she was going to try her best to do just that.

She was doing some last-minute packing when Kody called. "Hello." He heard the excitement in her voice which got him charged.

"Hey sweetheart. Are you just about ready? I figured we could head out around noon. I want to get up there early so we can get in as much time as possible. I have a lot planned when we get up there and want to make sure we get it all done, or at least as much as we can without me changing up on you."

Sunshyne knew what he meant. They could be watching a movie talking about getting something to eat, and before the movie ended he would come up with at least four different restaurants they were going to. "I don't care what we do while we're there. I am just looking forward to being away with you."

"Ok. Then we're good. I'm going to stop by the cleaners, and then I'm on my way to pick you up. I'd say give me about forty-five minutes, and I'll be there."

"Alright. I'll be sure to be ready."

They hung up the phone, and Sunshyne remembered a couple items she wanted to take with her. She knew no matter how many times she checked her bag she was going to have to run by the local mall or Walmart. She made sure she had her little black bag with her; she wanted to make sure they got the most out of their time alone.

***

Sunshyne was about to get comfortable and start watching one of the episodes of Queen Sugar she had saved on her DVR. She couldn't get enough of Kofi Siriboe, and she enjoyed the plot as well. Kody finally made it an hour and twenty minutes later and caught her during Me'shell Ndegeocello's opening song. She buzzed him up and asked him to have a seat on the couch while she grabbed her bag and used the washroom.

"Girl. I thought you would be ready by now."

"I am ready. I just need to use the bathroom before we get on the road, or you will be stopping as soon as we hit the highway."

"Alright. Hurry up, woman."

She twisted her face at him, "Hurry up from the man who said he would be here in forty-five minutes about an hour and a half ago."

"Why are you still here talking? Let's go already," he said in a playful tone.

Sunshyne was back and ready to go within in minutes. Kody took her bag, and they headed to the car.

"Have you eaten anything yet?"

"I ate breakfast with the kids so I'm not hungry."

He opened the passenger door, and then he put her bag in the trunk. As he sank into the front seat he thought to himself how he wanted this weekend to fabulous. He had a lot planned and hoped she would enjoy everything they were going to do.

He turned on his Compton's Most Wanted playlist to start out their trip. "You ready, Ms. Morris?

"Yes sir."

"Then let's get this show on the road." They set out for the highway to enjoy their weekend of fun.

ACKNOWLEDGMENTS

I would first like to thank my God for giving me the talents to bring my thoughts and ideas to life. I have made it to this place in life to be able to create my stories only through His graces and mercies. I am grateful for everyone on my team who has in one way or another contributed to making my books a success. I would like to thank my editor, Guernica D. Williams of After 6 Media, LLC. for your insight that helped expand and enhance my creativity. Thank you to everyone who has continued to support me from the very beginning of my journey. I hope that through the situations my characters experience, my readers will not only be entertained but that some will find hope, comfort or encouragement along the way.

I hope this story has lived up to what you have been waiting for. Please feel free to leave any reviews, comments or suggestions on my website at shellykewwrites.com. I look forward to hearing from you.

About the Author

Shelly Kew, born Nichelle Renee Askew was raised in Evanston, IL. She graduated Summa Cum Laude from Robert Morris University and has worked in the legal profession for over ten years. She has been writing as a hobby for years, until she finally decided to make her dreams reality and turn those writings into published work. Shelly Kew is creating stories her readers can relate to and portrays characters that are dealing with some of the same complex issues that are dealt with in everyday life.

Connect with Shelly Kew on:
Twitter: @AuthorShellyKew,
Facebook: Shelly Kew
Instagram: ShellyKew
Website: ShellyKewwrites.com

56853118R00090

Made in the USA
Columbia, SC
02 May 2019